Looking into the
Heavens

ROBERT CASPANELLO

Fulton Books
Meadville, PA

Published by Fulton Books 2023

ISBN 979-8-88731-128-9 (paperback)
ISBN 979-8-88731-129-6 (digital)

Printed in the United States of America

To my father, Joseph Caspanello.

Dad, I will always be looking into the heavens,
knowing that you are looking down on me.

CHAPTER 1

"Mom, I'm home!" he yelled as he made a beeline to his room.

Throwing his gym bag on the floor, he flicked on his PC, grabbed a change of clothes, and jetted to the bathroom. He was in luck; neither of his sisters was home yet.

It was a typical, hot July day in South Florida; Gary had gotten back from the school gym after summer weight training all afternoon and was exhausted. He had run eight miles prior to his workout and was glad to be out of his sweaty, smelly T-shirt and jump in the shower to recover. He was determined to be in better shape this year when football started, and nothing was going to stop him from making the team. He was the smallest on the junior varsity squad last year, which was not unusual, seeing that he was also younger than everyone else on the team. Having skipped fourth grade might have been beneficial to his mind, but his body needed some catching up. Besides, he knew there was a position for him on the varsity there for the taking. After all, he was a placekicker, and the varsity kicker had just graduated. But Gary wasn't taking anything for granted. He never forgot what his dad had taught him when he was ten years old: *Always do your best. It's not a matter of being good or bad, it's about being right. When you are right, good comes all by itself. Nothing in life is given, you have to go out and earn it.* The words rang clear to him today as it did back then. It was the last advice his father gave him prior to him dying four years earlier. He wasn't going to let him down. He was determined to make it happen.

Gary was stepping out of the shower and was drying off when there was a bang on the door. "Hey, your girlfriend is on vacation, and no one here cares how great you might smell, so hurry up! Steve's gonna be here any minute now!"

He wrapped a towel around himself and opened the door. There stood his older sister with that look of death in her eyes. Donna was a tall, blond, and beautiful young girl. Her appearance made her look much older than her seventeen years, but her attitude was all that of a teenage girl. Her body and her looks might present her a cheerleader type or an athlete, but anyone who knew her would ever tell her that. She could never be that kind of girl. That was too much work; she liked to cut loose and have fun when she could. Where Gary got the computer, she got the cell phone. Gary got books; she got CDs. She was far from stupid. She would crush them with your own special intellect and wit if they tried to stereotype her because of her hair color. They were opposite in a lot of ways, but the same in others. They were brother and sister, after all. She yelled because it was expected of her and he had rushed to get into the bathroom earlier to give her that reason to yell.

"What's the problem?" he said, still dripping wet and blocking the doorway.

"You're the problem. Steve will be here to pick me up, and you probably didn't even leave me any hot water."

"Oh, you want water? No problem, sis. Here." And with that he gave her a big hug, drying his wet hair on her face, neck, and shirt. She pushed him away, and he scrambled around her, making a bolt to his room. Unfortunately, Donna was too fast for him, and she was able to reach out and grab the towel as he ran by.

"Whoa, little brother, nice buns there!" she yelled laughingly as he slammed the bedroom door behind him. She had started to go in the bathroom when she saw his change of clothes on the sink. "Hey, Gary, don't you need this clean underwear?" She laughed.

Gary opened the door, wrapped now in a dry towel he had in his room, and said, "No, I have another pair, but go ahead, you can wear them on your date. Won't Steve be surprised when he *feels* them on you?" He closed the door just in time to intercept his clothes that were flying toward him.

"Gary," his mom called, "don't get too involved online yet. Dinner will be ready in fifteen minutes."

"Okay, Mom, I'm just going to check my mail."

2

Gary had just gotten his computer for his birthday in June, and it didn't take long for him to talk his mom into getting him an internet account. He wasn't sure at first if he was going to like it. His mom only agreed so he would have access to web information for his schoolwork. He did find it a good fill-in after Lynda dumped him at the beginning of the summer. He had never gotten around to telling Donna that he and Lynda had broken up. It happened so fast he was really caught off guard. He became withdrawn, not because she wasn't there, but because she left with the idea that it was a summer that they would not be a couple and would be open to other relationships. The past summers that she had spent with her father never presented these feelings, but then again, they had only been intimate with each other for the past year. Earlier, they were just best of friends, always there for each other. This time it was more of a betrayal. The computer was a godsend because it opened a new world for Gary to explore. The instant flow of any information was available to him. Gaming apps and music downloads filled in the gaps. Connecting with his school friends in online chat rooms gave him the distraction to get through the summer. He found making new friends online was easy, and made several from other parts of the country.

Clicking on his Internet Explorer, he noticed that he had one letter in the inbox. It was from one of his new friends, Kim, who was a regular in the chat room he hung out in. She was also fourteen and lived in Vermont, and an athlete also, so they had some things in common. The letter, unfortunately, was not good news. She was going to soccer camp on Monday and would be offline for two weeks. The letter was also an ultimatum that she would be online tonight at eight thirty and he had better be there. He was just sending his reply when his mom called him to dinner.

"Where's Carol?" Gary said as he sat down. Carol was his younger sister. She was eleven years old and a miniature version of her older sister. All attitude without the curves. But she was the baby, the special one, and she knew it.

"Carol is over at Jenny's house. She'll be back in the morning," Donna replied.

"So why do we have four plates on the table?"

"Hey, dweeb, I told you Steve was coming over."

"All right, he can help me with this new virtual game I'm having problems with."

"Don't think so! His date is with me, jerk. I didn't know you had homosexual tendencies?"

"Neither does he when you are with him, I'll bet!"

"Stop it, both of you!" Mom said. "You wonder why I don't ever bring a date over for dinner, with your kids home, talking to each other like that. And don't you think I don't see that you've got Carol talking the same way.

"Aww, come on, Mom, after a guy tastes your cooking, he won't complain about anything," Gary quipped.

"Well, unless Mom makes her famous stuffed cabbage and then breaks out the Pepcid AC—she'd lose him for sure," Donna added.

With that, they all laughed, even Mom; after all, she was where the kids got their sense of humor in the first place.

Just then, the doorbell rang, followed by three sharp knocks. Donna raced to the door to let Steve in. He was very predictable. He had the same mannerisms that he used since he was a small kid. But even at nineteen, he was still that little boy who grew up down the street Mom grew to love. Mom was usually the overprotective type, but with Steve and Donna, she was totally comfortable.

Donna had just set the salad on the table before going over to let him in. Just a quick kiss in front of Mom, though. They didn't want to give the wrong idea, like Mom was too naive to know. She wouldn't have hired him if she didn't think she could trust him.

"Hi, Mrs. Moran! We got the foundation in on the Taylor house today. Everything went good," Steve said with a broad but tired smile.

"Good, but let's not talk about work at the dinner table. That was one of John's biggest rules. Sit down and eat. Donna, can you get some napkins? And, Gary, how about waiting until we all sit down before you dive into the food?"

Gary stopped midbite, with a piece of lettuce hanging out of his mouth. He had scooped up some of the salad as soon as his sister put it on the table. He quickly chewed and swallowed. "Sorry, Mom, I have a lot to do after dinner."

"Oh, he must have an online date," his sister quipped. "Who is it tonight, Lisa or Kim?"

"Kim, as it's any of your business!"

"And what about Lynda? Does she know you are flirting behind her back?"

"Lynda doesn't care what I do behind her back or in front of her…or anything…we…broke up!"

With that, Donna became silent; she saw the pain in her brother's eyes when he said that. She knew Lynda was very special to her brother, and she had just unintentionally stabbed him with her remark there.

"Oh, I'm sorry. I didn't know. When did—"

Just then, Mom stopped her. "Donna, let's not talk about this now. Gary, what do you have on your hands? Go into the bathroom and wash them."

There really wasn't anything on his hands, but she also saw the pain and saw his eyes start to water. Her son needed an excuse to leave the table, and she gave it to him.

After dinner was over and the table had been cleared, Gary went to his room for a night of "flirting," as his sister had put it earlier. It bothered him that even though he and Lynda had broken up, he still felt guilty about the idea. He had no sooner sat down at his desk than there was a knock on the door.

It was Donna.

"Hey, Gary, can I come in? I want to talk to you a second."

"What? I thought you had a date tonight?" he said as he opened the door to let her in.

"I do, but Steve will wait. I'm sure Kim will also. Can we talk?"

"Yeah, sure, Kim won't be on till eight thirty. You really have Steve trained like some puppy."

"Yeah, but he loves it. So…hey, why didn't you tell me you broke up with Lynda?"

"I didn't break up with her, she broke up with me. She said because we were going to be away from each other for the summer, that we should break so we could see other people."

"What a bitch! She's been gone for two months now. When did she tell you this? Did she call?"

"No, she dumped it on me the day she left."

"You mean you kept this to yourself for eight weeks now?" Donna moved over to her brother and put her arm around his neck and squeezed it gently. "Hey, little brother, why do you keep these things to yourself like that?" With that, she gave him a big hug, and Gary returned the same. "You know that I will always be here for you to talk to. I'm not a total bitch."

As they broke their sibling embrace, Gary said, "Yeah, not a total one." They both laughed as Gary went flying onto the bed.

"But a bitch that can still throw your scrawny ass around. Don't you forget that! We'll talk more later. I have to rescue Steve from Mom."

"Later…and, Donna, thanks."

"No problem. Just don't let that ego grow faster than you do. Remember our promise."

She smiled and left, closing the door behind her. Gary lay back on his bed and closed his eyes. He remembered well the promise that he and his sister had made to each other. It was the day of his father's funeral. They vowed to always be there for each other and their little sister. They might have fought constantly, as all siblings do, but they loved each other nonetheless. It was what their father always said: *"Family sticks together. You can never turn your back on family, because your family should never turn their backs on you."*

John Moran was a loving husband and a good father. He worked as hard building his family as he did any building he erected. As a contractor and owner of a small but growing construction company, he had made quite a name for himself in the last twenty-five years in South Florida. One day, however, an accident changed all that. While he was inspecting a storm-torn structure after a tropical depression, it collapsed, killing him instantly. His loss would have been totally devastating for most families, but his legacy was his family. They were a close family, thanks to him. He was proud of them. Maria was his strength, a devoted wife and very well organized. She was a true partner in their relationship, at home and at work. Together they started a small company and built it into one of the leading custom home contractors in Dade County. It would have been no surprise to John that Maria was able to continue in their dream and be there for her children.

Donna was the splitting image of her mother. She was strong-willed and responsible. Even at thirteen years old, she had taken on the responsibilities at home to take the burden off her mother after her father's death. She had a special bond with her younger siblings. She knew that Mom couldn't always be there, so she promised to always be there for them. But she still was the big sister, which meant she was the boss, and she relished the role. So much so that Gary's nickname for her, Queen Bitch, was one of a term of endearment. She had to grow up fast emotionally as she did physically. When she was eight years old, she got this crush on this boy up the street, Steve, and devoted all her efforts to be around him. It wasn't until she entered high school that she was able to catch his desire for her. But for Steve, it wasn't just her beauty that got to him, but something more. He had known her for as long as he could remember. He grew up watching her grow up before him, but he never gave it a thought that she was anything more than some little girl in the neighborhood. That all changed in his junior year. When he started high school two years earlier than her, he grew past neighborhood happenings and lost track of his past friendships. But there she was, a new freshman that looked familiar to him. Was that Donna? He was totally amazed by her beauty and poise. She had that air of self-confidence and independence about her. She had, in the past two years, grown up much faster than he could have ever imagined. He wasn't looking at a little girl anymore; he was looking at a young woman. She handedly fended off the irritating boys her own age. She already knew these boys were too young for her; she already had her man all picked out. She saw Steve and gave him a smile of recognition and walked away. Fate had played its part that day, and the two would be together forever.

Where Donna was the responsible one and Carol the baby, Gary was always thought of by his sisters to be the favorite. After all, he was tested as being near genius at eight years old. He was reading by age two, knew how to add/subtract at age three, and at age six, was able to write concurrent sentences with uniform thought and meaning. He was a gifted child, but to his family it was they who were gifted for having him. He skipped fourth grade and entered fifth to challenge his learning ability further. It was suggested that he be enrolled in a special school for gifted children so that he could learn as much as his mind could fathom, but his parents would not have it. They knew he was special, but he really wasn't anything more than just a normal boy, and they did not want him to outgrow his youth. The decision to keep him in the public school system came with a lot of disconcertment from school administrators. They warned that his mind would always seek challenges and he would get bored easily in mainstream educational facilities. But his parents' concern was for Gary. What did he want to do? Did he want to grow up as some computer geek, which would isolate him from the other students? No. He should be with children his own age, should learn with them. As far as challenges, Dad had come up with an idea for that, and Gary jumped at it. Peewee football was the answer. Gary, being a smaller boy, always was pushed around and picked on, but he loved the idea of being able to get on the field and knock other guys around and not be worried about being beaten up. Yes, sports were the key to keeping his mind and his body challenged, allowing him to grow up like a normal kid. Mom was concerned about him getting hurt, but after looking at his enthusiasm, she knew she couldn't stop him. Those concerns were lessened the day he came home with the announcement that the coach was teaching him to be a placekicker.

Gary, despite his high IQ, was truly growing up as any other normal boy. *Normal* in the sense that he liked all the things boys liked. He played video games, rode his bike, played football, and went to the beach. He loved the ocean. He had learned to surf from his father, and he could lose himself at the beach from dawn to dusk if you let him. But no matter how fast his body was growing, his mind never stopped. He was a slim boy with some muscle tone. His brown eyes and shoulder-length dark-brown hair was contrasted by his wry smile. His medium-tan complexion was typical of any Florida youth who loved the outdoors. His attempt to maintain a "surfer" image during the summer, however, was always marred by his boyish looks and advanced vocabulary. In the fall, he would cut his hair short in readiness for the football season and take on a "preppy" appearance. He was always critical of the way he looked. In most instances, he was a young man still looking for a sense of identity. Because of the diverse attention he received, he always had trouble maintaining a lot of long-term friendships. His father's death had made him withdrawn, too, and shy at times, which made him somewhat antisocial to his peers. Being a year younger than his classmates didn't help either. On the positive side, though, it made him less appealing to the Miami youth gangs for their "membership." High school and football were very therapeutic to Gary. It had given him the self-confidence that he sorely needed. Online chatting was a new and inventive means to bring out the unique and charming personality that lay dormant within him.

At the age of twelve, he had started to show true signs of his boyhood when he discovered girls. Like with his older sister, Gary's first love had literally been in front of him all the time. After all, Lynda lived directly across the street from him. They were childhood pals, going back when they were both in diapers. Lynda, being an only child, and although a year younger, was always there with Gary. They did almost everything together. They grew up as friends, but it was inevitable that would grow into much more. It was just this past year that they became more intimate as puberty took hold.

Lynda was the direct opposite of Gary. She was a petite girl with short sandy-blond hair, blue eyes, and a broad smile. She was pretty in her own way, with a very outgoing personality. Her parents had divorced when she was three. Her main hobby was photography, which was not unusual, seeing that both her parents were career photographers. Her father traveled around the world doing nature shoots for everything from educational journals to magazine ad campaigns. Her mom owned an exclusive studio for fashion modeling used for catalog ads. She had learned at a young age how to use a camera and develop her own pictures, especially since her mom maintained a darkroom in their house. She had grown up to be very independent. She was a straight-C student even with Gary's feeble attempts to tutor her. The only thing they really had was the trust they had in each other. They always shared information, feelings, problems, whatever. So when both bodies started to change, it was not surprising that the changes were talked about between the two. Gary, however, always had the upper hand when it came to anatomical changes. After all, he had two sisters, and his mind had already touched on almost all the changes a female body could go through. He had found out later that wasn't always the case. Sure, he knew about breast getting bigger, the appearance of body hair, and the like. He even had the insight about menstruation after coming across a box of tampons in the bathroom when he was younger. But there were things they learned together.

The first time they kissed started as just an experiment. But the kiss was much more. It brought out feelings that the two had for each other, though they were too young to realize, and it was even harder to understand. Gary never forgot that moment. They were at a party on Miami Beach by a mutual friend of both their mothers. They broke away from what proved to be a very boring gathering, to the seclusion of the ocean shore. They walked barefoot down the surf and talked for about an hour under a starlit sky. Then, they came across two teenage lovers "making out" on the beach and quietly moved away to avoid interrupting them. But the sight stirred something inside both, and the conversation turned to kissing. After Gary conferred with his book-sense knowledge on kissing as to eyes open/closed, mouth open/closed, or with/without tongue, it was Lynda who said, "Let's just try it." Gary's logical mind gave way to her impulsive demeanor. They moved closer to each other and pressed their lips together. It lasted only a second, but after they parted, the look in Lynda's eyes told him to continue.

It was an hour later when they returned to the party. They had left earlier as friends but returned hand in hand as much more.

Gary's thoughts about Lynda and his fatigue from the day's activities took their toll on him, and he drifted quietly into a deep sleep.

"Gary! Gary, wake up!"

"Huh…what? Mom?"

"Get out of bed. Manny is here. Did you forget to tell me about your plans today?"

"Huh, what time is it?" He looked over to the clock and noticed it said eight thirty. Also noticing the light shining from his window, he knew it was morning. "Ah, shit, I must have fallen asleep. Kim is gonna be pissed!"

"She'll get over it. Now, get up and go brush your teeth and scrub that tongue a little bit also." She was referring to the expletive—that in his daze he forgot he was talking to his mom. "I'll make you some breakfast and keep Manny occupied, and then we will talk about what your plans are for today."

Gary quickly got up and rushed to the bathroom. It was empty. After completing his daily routine of personal hygiene, he went out to greet his friend.

"Hey, look who finally dragged his ass—ah, *butt*—out of bed."

"Thanks! Your sister wore me out last night. I needed the sleep."

"You wish you could get my sister—"

"That's enough, boys!" Mom called from the kitchen. She entered with a plate of waffles and a jug of orange juice and set them down on the table. "Okay, spill it. What do you think you were going to do today?" she said as she poured both boys a glass of juice.

"I got tickets to the Marlins game this afternoon, Mrs. Moran."

"Yeah, Mom, I told you we might go."

"Might go…and when was it decided that I said you could go? Gary, I have some work to do today, and I was counting on you to keep an eye on Carol. Or did you forget that I told you that?"

"Ah, Mom…" He caught himself when he saw the look on Mom's face. He already knew he had lost this round.

"Besides, you are supposed to cut the grass this morning. You should do it before it gets too hot."

With that, he knew that she had just made his plans for him for the day. Gary finally surrendered to his fate, and the boys quickly finished their breakfast and went outside so Gary could start his lawn work.

"Hey, that sucks you have to be stuck with your sister like that."

"Yeah, but fuck it, I'm going anyway."

"How you gonna do that?" Manny paused while looking at his friend's face. "Ah, shit, I know that look. Okay, what's your plan this time?"

"Look, if I know Carol, she's going to have Jenny here all day, so if I can talk her and Jenny into going to the game with us, then I can go."

"But we don't have tickets for them, how are we—"

"I have some money saved up, and the games are never sold out. We'll get two seats somewhere, let the girls have our tickets, and they can sit with your parents and we have the game to ourselves."

"Where do you come up with these ideas? You know you're going to get caught again. You always do."

"No, I don't, and hey, it's my ass, not yours. Let me handle it."

"Okay, it is your ass, but one of these days your genius bullshit isn't going to get you out of the shit you get into."

"The game isn't until one thirty. I will call you after I finish the lawn and I've talked to Carol."

"What if she doesn't want to go?"

"Leave Carol to me. She'll go. It will cost me, but she will go. Trust me." Gary turned. "Hey, I don't suppose you'd want to hang and help me out with the lawn, do you?"

"No way. I just did mine yesterday, bro. I did my time."

"That's okay. I'll handle it. I'll call you by eleven."

Manny jumped on his bike and rode back to his house.

The two had been friends for many years, and the Herta family was like a second home for him. Gary helped him a lot getting through algebra 1, and Manny helped Gary get through freshman year without getting hurt. Manny was five foot ten, two hundred pounds, and all muscle. He was a linebacker on the JV team with Gary.

As Manny rode off, Gary's mind was already at work on how to get his sister to come along. Like his older sister, she was very independent and could be very stubborn when she wanted to. Besides, there was always the Jenny factor. He knew Jenny had a small crush on him; maybe that would work in his favor. He went through all the scenarios in his head as he did his work. He knew he could make it work. This was his main vice. He loved to outthink any situation and make it work to his advantage. He was notorious for his scheming and planning, which had gotten him in and out of a lot of trouble in the past.

He was almost finished with the yard when a car pulled up the driveway. Gary, shirtless by this time, went over just as the doors flew open and out popped two laughing eleven-year-olds. Carol, pulling her backpack out of the back seat, had Jenny whispering in her ear. Carol whispered something back, and they both started giggling again.

"Hi, Mrs. Wright."

"Hello, Gary. Are you sure you are going to be able to handle these two hellions this afternoon? They have been acting like this all morning."

"Yeah, I guess my mom volunteered me," Gary said with a sigh. "Oh, Mrs. Wright, Manny's dad *was* going to take us to the Marlins game this afternoon. They have extra seats. Will it be okay with you if I take Jenny to the game with us?"

"Your mom didn't say anything about that. Did she say it was okay?" she asked quizzically. She was up on his reputation of his plans and schemes that usually were without parental approval, but Gary, regardless of his thrill-seeking, was always responsible when it came to involving others in his schemes. This one seemed harmless, so she figured to play along and watch his work on this con job she was about to get.

"Well, not yet. Manny was here an hour ago and told me about the extra tickets, so I figured I'd ask you first and then get ahold of my mom to ask her about Carol."

"Hmm, I see, and Mr. Herta is going to the game also?"

"Of course. He will go to the game whether we go with him or not. He will pick us up here at twelve thirty, and we should be home by five thirty."

"Okay, but how do you know if the girls want to go?"

Gary turned to the girls and looked at his sister with a stern look on his face, which transformed her face instantly into a sly-looking smile. She knew what her brother was up to, and she knew this was going to cost him also.

"Well, just don't stand there. Do you want to go or what?"

"I don't know, Gar. We were just going to hang out around the house today. It's too hot to go to the game today." She had him on the ropes. She was going to make him beg now. Donna had taught her well.

"Aw, come on, it's not that hot," Gary said as he was wiping the sweat from his neck. "You always said you wanted me to take you to a game, and now I'm taking you and you don't want to go." His voice got a little tense for a moment there, and he decided a change of tactics was needed. He looked at Jenny and smiled. "What about you, Jenny? Do you want to go to the Marlins game with me?" His inflection on "with me" was perfect.

She smiled and started to talk. "Yeah, I—"

Carol stopped her midsentence. "Wait a minute, Jen. We have to talk." With that, the girls moved back behind the car and whispered to each other. After about a twenty-second conference, Carol came back with a counteroffer.

"Okay, we will go, but Jenny is sleeping over, so you will have to let us use your computer to chat online tonight."

"Okay, deal, but only for an hour. And I pick the chat room."

"You know, I think both of you are going to be very good lawyers someday," said Mrs. Wright. "Okay, Gary, here's forty dollars for Jenny's share of the afternoon. Give Mr. Herta fifteen dollars for the ticket. The rest is for you to spend on you and the girls. Jenny, listen to Mr. Herta, and don't you girls wander. It's a big stadium. Don't get lost."

Jenny gave her mom a hug goodbye, and both girls scrambled into the house as she drove off. Gary went back to work with a broad smile on his face. It was working better then he figured so far—he got help with the funding, after all. Next stop was Mom. He knew he had to clear it with her now, or Mrs. Wright would mention it for sure later and he would be snagged.

He finished the lawn and rushed inside to get ready for the afternoon. He called Manny, telling him that everything was going as planned. He reminded him to let his father know that the girls had to come with them because they couldn't leave them behind.

He grabbed some clothes and a towel and headed for the bathroom. *Damn.* The door was locked.

"Hey, hurry up! I've got to get in there."

No answer. Just as he was about to bang on the door again, it opened and there stood Jenny. "Thanks for wanting to take us to the game today."

"Like I had a choice," he said in a disturbed voice. "Are you done in there?"

"Yeah, go ahead," she responded as she walked by to let him in. "Carol says you are going to try out for the varsity team this year. Think you are going to make it?"

"I don't know. Maybe."

"Whew, you do stink. Why don't you take a shower?"

"I'm trying to, if you would leave me alone."

Yes, he was good at playing people, especially girls. His sisters were good, but he had learned a lot from them, how to read them and take control when necessary.

He jumped in the shower and started to think of what to tell his mom.

*****

Back in Carol's room, she and Jenny were settling into their plans for the remaining day and the sleepover that night. Carol already had the radio blaring to the sounds of a local alternative rock station. The two of them had been inseparable most of their short lives. They were both two cheerful eleven-year-olds. Carol was proud of her long blond hair, which she displayed hanging freely down her back. She would never think of tying it back unless she was at her gymnastics class or swimming. Jenny, on the other hand, had short brown hair and a pudgy short stature. Both girls had the makings that destined them to be two very beautiful young women someday. But today, they were still eleven and in no real rush to grow up yet.

They readied themselves for the hot July afternoon at the stadium.

Gary was just putting on his socks and sneakers when the phone rang.

"I got it! It's Mom!" he called out. Mom and Donna had cell phones; Gary did not. Like the bathroom, the phone was another commodity that he had to complete with his little sister. He had called his mom as soon as he got out of the shower and left a quick message, so he had been waiting eagerly for her call to finish off his plan.

"Hi, Mom," he said directly as he picked up the phone.

"Okay, Gary, what's wrong?"

"Nothing's wrong, Mom. What makes you say that?"

"Okay, then you want something. Spill it. I have to get back to my work."

"Well, remember that Marlins game I wanted to go to this afternoon? Well, Mrs. Wright said it was okay to take Jenny to the game with us. Manny's parents are both going, and we can get two extra tickets for Jenny and Carol. Can we go? Please?"

"Hmm, sounds like you have this all planned out, so tell me, Einstein, what are the money plans? I know you already have that worked out. So...?"

"Yeah, that's no problem. I have money saved, Carol has her money, and Mrs. Wright gave me forty dollars because I offered to take the girls. They wanted to go, so can we go, please?"

"Okay, call Manny and tell him it's all right. When are you leaving, and what time will you be home?"

"Manny will be here in about five minutes, and we should be home by five."

"Well, you better get going and get ready. Take care of your sister and Jenny."

"Mom, I'm already ready. And here come the girls. They're all set to go." He gave Carol a thumbs-up and a smile to let her know that he was successful again on getting the one-up on his mother.

"You know, one of these days I might not go along with all your scheming, little man. Then what are you going to do?"

"I don't know. I'll think of something then." He hesitated as he heard a car out front and then a horn sound. "Mom, I got to go. That's Manny. Don't worry, I'll take care of the girls. Don't forget, I'm the man of the family now."

"Yes, I know. Too much of a man for a little boy, if you ask me. Okay, go and have fun. Don't load up on garbage. I will have dinner waiting for all of you when you get home."

"Okay, Mom. Bye. Love ya."

CHAPTER 2

It was five thirty when the young baseball fans arrived home. Even though exhausted from the day's activities and the Florida sun, they all were in fairly good spirits. The girls came rushing in and went right to Carol's bedroom.

"I got first dibs on the bathroom!" Gary announced as he walked in the front door. "Hey, Mom, we're home!"

"Too late. Donna is in there already. You will have to wait. Sit down here and tell me how the game was. Who won?"

"We did. Good game too. Score was 5–4. We pulled it out in the ninth."

"Great! How were the girls? How many fights did you two get into?"

"None. The dweeb and her friend were pretty normal today?"

Just then, the bathroom door opened and out pranced Donna, dressed in her bathrobe, drying her hair with a towel. "Oh, you're back? Did ya have fun babysitting today?"

"Oh, real fun, but it was easy. Those girls are as horny as you are. They did more guy-watching than the game."

"Look at the alternative: you and Manny or the rest of the stadium. My girls aren't stupid!" She turned and went into her room to get dressed. Gary quickly ran to get into the bathroom.

During dinner, Mom announced that there would be a family meeting after dinner was over and everyone was to put all plans for the evening on hold. Family meetings were usually eventful in the Moran house. It usually meant that Mom was going to set down certain rules, inform them of upcoming happenings, or anything on which the consensus of the family was not to like. Dinnertime passed quickly with uneasy anticipation. The table was cleared, and Jenny exited to her friend's room to await the meeting's outcome.

"Okay, this isn't going to be easy for all of you, but… Gary, this letter came today. It's for your benefit, but it's going to affect everyone, so read it out loud."

Gary took the letter from the envelope. He unfolded it and began to read:

> *South Central Catholic High School*
> *1325 Riverside Blvd.*
> *Riverside, FL 33460*
>
> *It is with great honor to inform you that your application for your child Gary Moran for enrollment on the upcoming school year has been accepted. We appreciate your interest in our educational program and would like to thank you for your perseverance over the years while waiting for an opening to be available.*
>
> *Please fill out the attached information sheets and return them to us as soon as possible. Please call (561) 555-8200 for any questions.*
>
> *Sincerely,*
> *Father Joseph Abernathy*
> *Principal*

There was a moment of silence, and then Gary was the first to speak.

"No way! Does this mean I'm not going back to South Kendall High this year? No, Mom, you can't… I mean, I'm not going…" He started to stammer. His mother, putting her hand on his on the table, stopped him from going on.

"Gary, you listen to me a second. Your father and I put you on the waiting list for this school when you were eight years old. Your dad always wanted the best for you, and this is one of the finest college preparatory schools in the state."

"I know the school, Mom, but what about football? I was going out for the varsity this year. And what about the drive up and back from Palm Beach every day? It's two counties away!"

"Well, first, this school has a very good football team, and you can still try out to get on the team there. And as far as traveling..." She paused and took a deep breath, then said, "We won't have to. We are going to move up to Riverside. Isn't that great?" She looked at her daughters. Her attempt at levity, however, didn't work, as they had just now discovered how this all affected them.

"Hey, wait a minute. Are you telling us that because the genius here gets accepted to some brain school, we all have to move? This is bullshit, Mom!" Donna said angrily as she stood up, kicking the chair out while doing it. Carol, whose eyes were starting to water, just sat there quietly, stunned, not able to speak. Although, even if she could at that point, she wouldn't get the chance, knowing that Mom and Donna were about to argue.

"Sit down, young lady, and watch that attitude! Now, we are going to move, and that is that." She stopped to regain her composure as Donna knew at that point to back down a little and picked up her chair and sat back down. "I know that maybe I should have discussed it with you, but since your father died, I have had to make a lot of changes for the benefit of the family, and I've had to do things that may not be all too acceptable to all of you. I am sorry that I had to dump this on you like this, but I had forgotten all about applying to that school. And then the letter came today..." Her voice became rough as she fought back the tension of the moment. "You are all growing up so fast. I wish I could slow things down and make things go easier for all of you, but I can't. I need all of you to help me... help us get through all this. Please understand, I can't let your dad's dreams die just because he did."

She sat down, shaken by her speech.

Donna got up and leaned over to hug her mother.

"We understand, Mom, but what about our friends here? And Steve, what am I supposed to tell him?"

"Does Steve love you?"

"Yes, and I love him."

"Okay, then it shouldn't matter where you live. That love will always be there. And you know Steve will follow you anywhere if nothing more than to get my cooking." She paused. "Carol, you've been pretty quiet there. Don't you want to curse me out for this too?"

"Yeah, Mama, I would, but I'd probably get the soap for saying what I think right now." Carol's response put a small smile on everyone's face, except for Gary's.

He was reading the letter repeatedly, taking in what his mother had said. The letter said, "Mr. & Mrs.," and his mom said that it was his father's plan that he go there. His mind was moving, trying to figure it all out. He was looking at all the reasons to stay but only one to go. This was his dad's plan for him. He knew of the school's reputation. It was a small private school high on the scholastic merits of its graduates but still had a decent athletic program for a school its size. The JV football team he was on just beat them last season. He knew how important this was to his dad for him to have planned like this so far ahead for him. He equally knew how important it was to his mom, too, for her to make such a drastic change in all their lives just to see that those plans were followed through. His decision was hard but altogether an easy one to come to once he thought it all out.

"Gary… Gary…are you okay?" his mom said, bringing him back to his senses. "You got that look on your face again."

"I'm okay, Mom. So when do we move?" he blurted out, to the amazement of his sisters.

"Mom, I think he's in shock. Gary, just like that, you're giving in?" Donna moved over to her brother in total disbelief.

"Hey, I'm fine. Stop looking at me like that. I just figured, if Dad wanted me to go there, then I'm going."

Carol was doing her own thinking and decided to add to the discussion. "Ah, Mom, where are we gonna live up there?"

"Well, the first thing on Monday, I'll be meeting with a realtor to put this house on the market and start looking for something up in Palm Beach County close to the school. But in the meanwhile…" She took a deep breath and watched as her children's faces turned to worry in anticipation of what they knew was the inevitable. "We will be moving in with your aunt Connie."

"Ah, Mom, I knew that somehow Aunt Connie will be part of all this," Donna said disdainfully. "I suppose that this means we will have to be going back to church every Sunday?"

"Probably, but that might help curb that wild mouth of yours. It wouldn't hurt for all of you to get a little God every week. Come on, all of you, it's only temporary. I talked to her today as soon as I got the letter. She can't wait to see all of you. Gary, you will have to share a room with Frank, and you girls will have to share the guest bedroom."

"Mom, no way! I can't share a room with her—she snores. I'd rather sleep on the couch!" Carol announced.

"Sound okay to me," Donna replied.

"We are not going to do this! Both of you, stop it, now. You will share a room and learn to tolerate each other. Like I said, this is temporary, so try to get along until I can find a house that will suit us."

"Okay, Mom, I will...hey, am I going to this school also?" Donna added.

"No, you and Carol will be going to public school."

A small smile was seen on Gary's face. Donna walked over to her brother and applied a soft headlock on him. "What are you smiling about, little bro? Who's gonna watch over you without me there?" Gary, knowing his sister's weakness, reached up and started to tickle her under her arms, so she released him laughingly.

"I'm not that little anymore. I'm sure I can handle it without you easily."

"Oh, Mom, are you sure it's a good idea to release this horny little boy on all those innocent Catholic girls there?"

"Ah-hmm, you are one of those innocent Catholic girls, remember? You should pity your brother if they are anything like you, young lady!" Mom's comment stopped Donna, but Gary's mind never stopped, as he was still thinking and trying to gather information.

"So, Mom, you never answered me before. When do we move?"

"Well, I told your aunt that we will be moving up next Saturday, so you have a week to get together all essentials, and, girls, I mean essentials that you need. Everything else, you will be coming back at times to help box up and get ready to move after we have a place to move it all too. Gary, your computer will have to stay, dear, I'm sorry. There really is no room for you to set it up, and Aunt Connie doesn't have internet, so you won't be able to get online anyway."

"What about you, Mom? You haven't said anything about where you are going to sleep up there," Gary interjected. "Her house isn't that big."

"Well, son, I'm going to stay here until the house is sold or we move into the new one. You know most of our business is down here in Dade. Eventually, I will commute back and forth every day. I may even consider moving the office up there. We'll see."

"So why do we have to move up there now? I'll stay here with you until you find something up there," Donna volunteered happily.

"No, I've talked to Connie and have given it some thought, and we think it would be better that you all move up there and get adjusted to living up there in the next few weeks before school starts. Besides, we must establish residency for both you girls in order to get you in the public school system, and I don't want either of you starting a school year down here and then transferring up to Riverside a couple of months in the semester. Okay, any more questions? Good, then the meeting is over. Donna, kitchen. Carol, go tell Jenny everything she couldn't hear through the door. Gary, come here and give your mother a big hug."

The girls took off to their duties, and Gary went over to his mom to hug her.

"Thank you, son, for making this easier for me. Your dad would be so proud of you, and I'm so proud of you." She held her son tight, holding back the tears. "Now, go get your computer on. I understand you have an arrangement with the girls for an hour of online chatting."

Gary booted his computer and navigated his regular chat room. He figured he had about thirty minutes before Carol and Jenny finished talking about the move and all. Almost immediately upon coming online, he received an instant message from one of his online friends. It was Kim.

Chickee89: *WHERE THE HELL WERE YOU LAST NIGHT!!!*

Pkicker: *Sorry, I fell asleep.*

Chickee89: *FELL ASLEEP!!! WOW, NOW I KNOW HOW IMPORTANT I AM!*

Pkicker: *Hey, I said I'm sorry, I ran 8 miles yesterday afternoon and was wasted last night, so chill now, and stop YELLING!!!*

Chickee89: *ok, I forgive you this time but watch it next time.*

Pkicker: *Oh, I'm scared now, whatcha going to do, come down here and kick my ass.*

Chickee89: *Naw, you'd like that too much. LOL.*

Pkicker: *Yeah, I would but by the time you get here, I won't be here anymore.*

Chickee89: *What's that supposed to mean?*

Pkicker: *My mom just broke it to us that we are moving up to Riverside, Florida.*

Chickee89: *where the hell is that? Why do you have to move?*

Pkicker: *It's in Palm Beach County; I got accepted to this private Catholic school up there.*

Chickee89: *Cool. So, what's the problem, you don't want to go?*

Pkicker: *Well, yes and no. I had a good chance of starting on the varsity team this year and all my friends are here. But my dad applied for me before he died so I have to go.*

Chickee89: *Can't you just say no and tell your mom you don't want to go.*

Pkicker: *No, not really. You don't know my mom, but it's a good school so we all have to move. My sisters are pissed.*

Chickee89: *Yeah, I can just imagine. Hey, what about Lynda? Are you going to tell her you're mov-*

ing or just let her find out on her own when she gets back after the summer?

Pkicker: *Fuck her, let her find out when she gets back. Hey, I bet she will be pissed off when she finds out I'm gone.* LOL

Chickee89: *Yeah, she will, that will teach her to dump ya like that.*

Pkicker: *yeah, wow, thanks, now I feel better about moving.* ☺

Chickee89: *Hey, that's what friends are for.*

Pkicker: *Yeah, I owe ya.*

Chickee89: *Yup, you do, so where's that poem you promised me?*

Pkicker: *I got it done. I will email it to you before I get offline tonight.*

Chickee89: *You better. I leave for soccer camp in the morning, so I will check my mail before I go. I have to get off now. Email me. Bye-bye.*

Pkicker: *Ok, I will. bye.*

Just then, there was a knock on the door. "Hey, Gary, we're ready to chat now. Can we come in?"

Gary opened the door but blocked their entrance. "No, not yet. Give me about ten minutes. I'm not done yet. I'll call you when I'm ready for you."

"Well, hurry up. When we said an hour, we didn't mean between eleven and midnight." Carol was playing tough with her big brother, showing off for her friend's benefit.

"Don't worry, you won't. Now, leave me alone so I can finish my mail." He closed the door and went back to his computer. Gary clicked on the mail icon to send Kim his poem.

Dear Kim,

I didn't get a chance to tell you, but I will be moving next weekend. We are moving in with our aunt

*until Mom finds a house up there. I'm not going to
be able to bring my computer, so I won't be online
for a while. Here is the poem I wrote. I hope you like
it. Try to email me before you leave tomorrow. Have
fun at soccer camp.*

Looking into the Heavens

*I am looking into the heavens, into the stillness of the night
My mind is at a gentle peace to behold such a sight
In my quiet slumber while my body is at rest
My dreams come alive with wonder; these times are at their best
All at once I am awakened, staring blankly into space
I find myself just lying there alone in a cold, dark place
Time passes by so slowly as my fears grow so fast
Minutes and seconds click on by; how much longer can this last
As my mind begins to wander; my heart starts to race
I have to find my way back there, back to that wondrous place
As sleep returns to take my lead, the silent loneliness all around
It moves so quickly to engulf my soul, no escape is to be found
In the distance a sound erupts, a gentle voice as it nears
It's calm and peaceful tone does sing, chasing away my fears
From the darkness a light appears, brightening up this place
I stand watch as you approach me, my soul held captive by your face
Through your eyes I see the path back to that wondrous sight
Once again, I am looking into the heavens, into the stillness of the night*

*Bye,
Gary*

He signed off and signed back on under a different screen name
he had set up for his sister's use. The last thing he was going to do was
let Carol talk to his online friends. He called them in and left them
alone to chat.

26

CHAPTER 3

As the plane rolled slowly toward the terminal, Jerry was silently applauding his success over the past three days. As the seat belt light went off, he quickly grabbed his overnight bag from the compartment above and made his way into the procession to exit the airplane. He turned on his phone as he walked and instantly received the text he was waiting for. *Package was released. Everything went as planned.* Another successful operation with a good payday at the end. He made his way through the crowds and proceeded to baggage claim. Still holding his cell phone, he quickly called to confirm his ride was waiting for him in the parking garage as planned. It would still be another hour before he would get through customs, but he needed to know that she was there to pick him up to keep on schedule.

Lauren hung up the phone and returned it to her back pocket. She closed the car door and walked to the exterior wall of the parking garage to light her cigarette to pass the time. It was a typical hot day, as normal for July in Texas. The breeze, for what was blowing that day, proved to be every bit of the 105-degree temperature the local weatherman said it was going to be. She was not used to it, having grown up in Vermont. She and Jerry had been together for almost three years. She would do anything for him. As hot as it was, she arrived early and waited as she was expected to do.

Four cigarettes later, Jerry was walking toward her, bags in tow. She hurried to the car, opened the trunk for him so he could load his suitcase. She greeted him with a big smile and a kiss, helped him load the trunk, and then handed him the keys. They quickly made their way to the exit and out to the expressway.

"Well, baby, we did it again. Everything went off without any problems…again. Did you miss me?" Jerry said as they drove off.

"Of course I did! I still don't know why I couldn't go with you."

"We went over this already. It's important that each phase of the operation must be handled individually. We stick to the plan and we minimize the risk of getting caught. Besides, you know the others will not be too cool on us both leaving the country when I collect the money."

"Yeah, I understand, but when are we going to take that break so we can enjoy some of that money?"

"We are right now. As soon as we get to the bank and close out the accounts, we can take off for Myrtle Beach. We have to close down for the next two weeks, anyway, to let things settle a bit before the next job."

"Why didn't you tell me that? I would have liked to get prepared a bit."

"Sorry, baby, there wasn't time. Look, we get the money and you can go shopping tonight, but you must pack tonight also, because the flight takes off at 8:05 tomorrow morning. I got the tickets four weeks ago. I wanted to surprise you with the trip."

"You bastard!" she yelled but then quickly smiled. "Have I told you how much I love you?"

"I think you just did. Did you put all your contacts on hold?"

"Yeah, everything is on hold for a couple of weeks. We have to postpone the Miami project for now. It changed locations on us."

This was not something Jerry wanted to hear. Disgusted with the bad news, he kept his composure and switched his thinking on how to rebound from the change in plans.

"Okay, we will go over it all when we get to Myrtle. Make sure you pack the files on the other projects, and I will decide on which one we are best ready to take on."

Jerry changed lanes to prepare to exit the freeway. He took out his phone and speed-dialed a number. "Yeah, it's me. I'm on the way to the bank. We meet at the warehouse at two thirty. Make sure Miguel shuts down all the IP addresses and destroy all paperwork on this operation. Nothing should be at the warehouse when I get there. Comprende, amigo? Good. See you then." He shut off his phone and handed it to Lauren. She opened the back and removed the battery, and then the sim card. She took a small envelope out of her purse marked with a *J*, removed a new sim card and replaced it with a new one, and placed the battery in the phone. She repeated the procedure with her phone next, putting both old sim cards in one envelope.

Jerry pulled into the bank parking lot, which was right off the expressway exit, and parked. As he went inside the bank, Lauren opened the trunk, removed the metal shears, and cut both sim cards in half. She then walked across the street to the gas station, depositing some of the pieces of the cards in the outside trash cans, and went inside to buy another pack of cigarettes, where she threw the rest away in the trash bin next to the soda fountains. She walked back to the car to await Jerry's return.

CHAPTER 4

The next week was very hectic. There were friends to say goodbye to, clothes to pack, and plans to make. Of course, Steve was there every minute, helping out when he wasn't at work. Finally, the big day came, and they packed up the company pickup truck and car and were off to Riverside. It was a small town outside of Lake Worth, just ninety-seven miles north where they were living now. They pulled up to Aunt Connie's house around ten thirty, and as they began to unload the vehicles, out from the house came their aunt, followed by their cousin Frank. Aunt Connie was a very boisterous and personable woman. She would talk for long periods of time, if you let her, without ever running out of things to say. She was extremely religious, which at times was more than Gary and his sisters could stand. After all the hugging and kissing was done with, the vehicles were unloaded, and they all started to get settled.

Frank was a year older than Gary and was always in some kind of trouble. He was smarter than he ever let on with people, but he liked to play the stupid role a lot just to be different. With his rebellious and adventurous attitude, he was a handful for his mother all by himself. Now with Gary and him together, there would be no telling what would happen.

"So, Frank, how's this school I'm going to? Do you like it?"

"Yeah, it's okay. The teachers are strict, especially the nuns, but the girls there…well, they make up for all the bad shit. Wait until you meet Barbara. You'll see what I mean."

The boys continued talking the rest of the day, until Gary's mom came to say goodbye and told them both to behave for her sister. She kissed her son and her nephew before leaving and closed the door behind her.

"Connie, I hope you can handle those two together. You know how much trouble they get into apart. Just imagine what will happen now they will be together for the next couple of months."

"Oh, don't worry. I've been able to stay up with Frank's wayward behavior. Maybe having Gary around will slow him down a bit."

"Don't bet on it. Gary has his own devil in him. He keeps it well hidden, but when he lets it loose, watch out! Of course, now I have noticed that since he has started to notice girls, he has been a little less troublesome. They are growing up so fast."

"Yes, that they are. Hey, you better get going. You still have to drive back home."

The two sisters said goodbye, and Mom left to drive back down to Miami. Her mind was on her children. Was she doing the right thing? "Yes!" she told herself repeatedly on the way home. This was the right thing to do. Selling the house wasn't going to be easy. John had built that house for her, but he also helped build this family, and it was strong. It didn't matter where they lived, as long as they were together; the memory of her husband would always be there.

*****

The next morning, the children all woke up to the smell of pancakes and bacon. As they sat down at the table, their aunt laid out the day's itinerary. First, they were all going to Sunday Mass at ten o'clock. The girls were going to help her move some things around the house to make it more comfortable for them, while the boys took care of the lawn work.

"You know, Gary, Frank has a pretty good lawn business going on here. What are you up to, twelve lawns, that you take care of now? Now that you are here, you both can make some good money this summer."

Gary was a little dismayed at the suggestion that he help his cousin cut lawns the rest of the summer, but he remembered his mom told him to bear with the shortfalls of the stay there. He guessed this was going to be one of them.

"Sure, Aunt Connie. Frank and I will rake in the cash. That is, if Frank needs my help." He sat back and waited for a reprieve from his cousin.

"That will work great for me. Between the two of us, we can knock off four lawns a morning and have the afternoon to hang out and cool down," Frank came back saying, to the disappointment of his cousin. "Besides, we can only do them on Tuesday, Thursday, and Saturday. We have summer football conditioning at the school on Monday, Wednesday, and Friday. You do still plan on working out for football, don't you?"

"Oh, yeah, you know it! So how good is the varsity kicker this year? Do I have a shot at taking him on?"

"Actually, no chance at all. He was a starter last year, and he's a senior this year, so you might be better off planning to play JV for another year. But we all try out for varsity, and then they split us up from there. There's always a chance."

"Okay, boys, stop the chatting and eat. We have to leave in thirty minutes for church," Aunt Connie interjected.

*****

The Moran children started to adjust to their new life in Riverside. Gary continued his summer workout program with his cousin at his new school. He started to meet new friends. His size presented him to his new "teammates" at first to be somewhat of a joke. Even his new coach looked at him with puzzlement. Gary knew he had a lot to prove here if he was ever going to make them all take him seriously. He was always up to the challenge.

"Hey, young man, come here a second!" yelled Coach Lewis to this new guy running and sweating with his players. Gary knew this was the opportunity to make it count. Without little hesitation, he turned to run to his new coach.

"What's your name, boy, and what are you doing running around my track?"

"Gary Moran, sir. I'm getting in shape to try out for your football team, sir."

"Are you now? At what position, might I ask?"

"Placekicker, sir."

"A kicker, eh? Well, what makes you think a freshman like you can handle a position like that?"

"I'm a sophomore, sir. I just moved here from South Miami. I was on the South Kendall High's JV team last year, sir. I know I can handle the job."

The coach looked down at this small boy and was quite impressed with his cockiness. What he lacked in size, he seemed to pick up with enthusiasm and confidence. But this was a coach that looked for more than that in his athletes. He expected performance. "Okay, Moran, what was your stats for last year?"

"I was 15 for 15 in extra points, 6 for 7 in field goals."

"Impressive. And what was the longest field goal you made last year?"

"I kicked a 36-yarder against your JV team last year. I missed a 41-yarder in that same game."

"Yeah, I remember that game…so that was you, huh? Well, then, we are just going to see about beefing you up a bit, son. Get back to your workout and I will see you at tryouts in three weeks."

Gary went back to his running. Coach Lewis went back to the locker room, where he was met by one of his assistant coaches, Mr. Parr.

"So, Chuck, did you meet that Moran kid?"

"Yeah, he's a cocky and polite little bastard, but as first impressions go, he might fit in. He told me how he beat your team last year," the coach said laughingly. "He's running too much. Go out and work with him. Find out what he eats and get him to eat more of it. He's too damn skinny. He needs to get on a high-protein diet so he can bulk up a bit more. Then get him working more in the weight room on strength conditioning than just running around the track and burning calories."

"Oh, yes, sir…hey, you must really like this kid."

"Yeah, something about him just tells me he's going to fit in good in this school."

Meanwhile, Gary and Frank were taking a breather from their laps. "So, Gary, what did you think of Coach Lewis?"

"Damn, it was like talking to a lawyer under cross-examination… I think he was just sizing me up."

"For what? Why do you say that?"

"Well, first, he called me a freshman, but his inflection when he said it told me he knew I wasn't a freshman. Also, he asked me for my stats. I told him I was on the JV team last year. Never told him I played, but he assumed I had stats. He probably already knew what they were. And then I baited him by telling my play against his JV team last year, and all of a sudden, he remembers that game and remembers me…he was checking me out."

"Gary, it's not a good thing to go around fucking with the coach's head…you're gonna get your ass into trouble. Especially Coach Lewis."

"No way! I can avoid trouble and get out of trouble faster than I can make it around this track—who's this guy coming toward us?"

"That's Coach Parr. He's the JV coach. He's a real asshole, so don't go pissing him off. You might be playing for him this year," he whispered to his cousin. "Hi, Coach, how ya been?"

"Fine, Frank. Nice to see you getting in shape for this year's season early. So this is your cousin, Gary, isn't it? You really did some damage against us last year at Kendall High."

Gary looked at his cousin with a glance which says, "I told you so."

"Yes, Gary Moran's the name, kicking's my game." That was corny, he thought as he extended his hand to the coach. "Sorry about last year, Coach, but I was on target that game. But this year, I'm all yours. I'll make it up to you."

"That's okay, Gary. I can never fault a player for doing his best on the field, for or against us. We must work on putting a little meat on those bones there. Let's sit down here a moment to go over some workout requirements…"

Coach Parr finished his nutritional training session and went on his way. The boys were finished for the day and proceeded home.

Gary got his first taste of his new school today. He went home with a better sense of security and self-confidence of his new life here. He began to truly believe that this was indeed the best thing for him.

CHAPTER 5

This was the day. The first day of football practice at his new school and he was a bit nervous. There must have been close to a hundred guys trying out. He, of course, was the smallest. Coach Lewis and his regiment of assistants marched into the gym promptly at 9:00 a.m., ready to start the new year. After everyone was signed in, they all hustled out into the 85-degree Florida morning air. Two hours later, after a barrage of exercises, running, jumping, rolling, squatting, agility drills, and then more running, the boys walked into the locker room exhausted and drained from their first of many tests of early manhood. The day was what he expected. The coaches could tell the ones who were not going to make it after a workout like that. Gary got through it with little difficulty. He felt good. He quickly showered and got dressed and had to wait for Frank to catch up. Steve was coming up from Miami and was going to the beach with his sister. He had had very little opportunity this summer to enjoy the ocean. He didn't want to miss out on this chance.

As Frank and he started out to the parking lot, they were chased down by Barbara along with some of her cheerleader friends.

"Hey, Frankie, wait up!" she yelled.

"Hi, Barb—"

His words were stopped short with the lunging kiss she planted on him.

"Ohhkay! I missed you too!" he said after he caught his breath.

"Where are you two running off so fast? Oh, hi, Gary."

"Duh…we are going to the beach today, remember? I asked you if you wanted to go, but you have shopping, which is more important."

"Oh, that's right. Hey, Gary, these are my two friends, Karen and Michelle. This is Frank's cousin, Gary."

"Hi, Gary! I've heard about you. You played for South Kendall last year. I was cheering at that game. You were the kicker, right?" Karen remarked.

"Yeah, that was me. I remember seeing you there too."

"Oh, yeah, right. How can you remember seeing me?"

"Hey, I was only in the game a few times. The rest of the time, I was checking out the opposing team's cheerleaders." He smiled at Karen. "You were the one who did that somersault and landed into a split. That's kinda hard to forget. You were hot."

"Damn, you were paying attention. That's a good quality for a guy. Are you going to Barbara's party on Saturday?"

"No. I haven't been invited…yet," he said with a small smile.

"Well, you are now. I'm inviting you as my date…that is, if you want to go?"

"How can I refuse an invitation from someone as beautiful as you?"

"Oh, and he's a charmer too. You didn't tell me that, Barb."

"Didn't know. Too bad it doesn't run in the family," Barbara said, grinning at Frank.

"Hey, now…anyone who looks this good doesn't need charm," Frank came back to his defense.

"Hell, you better let them go, girl. Frankie's going to need the ocean to soak that swelled head of his," Michelle added, getting into the conversation.

"Yeah, get going. Call me tonight. We have to be going too. Here comes Michelle's mom and Patti now. We are ready to shop," Barbara said as she gave her boyfriend a goodbye kiss. "Have fun at the beach, and remember, look, but don't touch!"

As the girls were walking away, Gary was quite pleased with himself having been asked out by Karen. She was a very beautiful girl with an outgoing personality, and very energetic. As he watched them, memories of his old school drifted away and were replaced with all the new experiences he started to imagine of his new life. He could not help but notice their friend Patti standing outside the car.

There was something that hit him about her. He wasn't sure what it was, but he just became fixed on her appearance there on this sunny Florida day.

He was brought back to reality with a loud beep from Steve's car as he arrived to pick him up.

"Well, I can see you are going to like going to this school, little brother," Donna said as the boys climbed into the back seat. "Oh, those poor girls! If they only knew what they're in for."

"Hey, one of those 'poor girls' just asked Gary out. Cuz has a date for Saturday night," Frank quickly remarked.

"From one of those girls? All right, Gary! Now that's really moving up from Lynda," Steve said.

Donna quickly pinched Steve's leg to point out his indiscretion of mentioning Lynda at that moment.

"Well, he deserves better than Lynda," she added quickly. "And you can just stop looking at those girls right now. I'm all the woman you need to be looking at." She looked back at her brother and winked, giving her own special approval of his new "friend."

Gary smiled back. He was in too good a mood to let the thought of Lynda ruin this day. He made it through his first day of practice, got a date for the weekend, and was on the way to the beach to surf. Life couldn't be better at that moment.

Meanwhile, back at the house, Carol was spending some quality time with her aunt when the phone rang.

"I got it, Aunt Connie!" Carol yelled before picking up the phone. "Hello."

"Hi, Carol? It's Lynda. How's it going? Is Gary there?"

"Oh, hi, Lynda… Gary's at practice now. How did you get this number?"

"I had it. Gary gave it to me last Christmas when you went up there for the weekend, so I could call him then. I had it in my book. So when is he getting home?"

"He won't be home till late. Donna and Steve were picking him up after practice and taking them to the beach. Knowing Gary, he will surf until the sun goes down."

"You got that right. So what happened? Why did you all move?"

"Gary got accepted to this school up here."

"Damn, that sucks."

"Sucks for who? You?" She couldn't hold back anymore. "You should have thought about that before you dumped him."

"Hey, sorry, girl. I did what I thought was right. Don't go giving me that attitude. Just tell Gary I called. I left him several messages online, but he doesn't even read them."

"He can't. His computer's not set up. He can't get online until we move into our own home."

"Well, that sucks again. Well, anyway, can you tell him I called?"

"Sure. He could use the laugh." And she hung up the phone. She couldn't stand talking to her any longer. She wrote down the message and went out the back door to her aunt.

Several hours later, the weary beachgoers arrived home. Gary was really wiped out with all the day's activities. The boys slumbered in and went right to their room to change. They were followed minutes later by Donna and Steve, who were stuck cleaning the sand from the car.

"Hey, we're home, Aunt Connie… Carol?" Donna called out upon entering the front door. She heard nothing. "Where is everyone?" Just then, she heard the back door opening and heard her sister's voice. Carol and her aunt appeared coming through the kitchen, laughing. They were dressed in bathing suits and half-wet.

"Oh, hi, Donna! I didn't' hear you come in," Aunt Connie said. "Where are the boys?"

"They are getting changed. What have you two been doing all day? And why are you all wet?"

"We were just out back hanging out and sunbathing back there. Aunt Connie grabbed the hose and soaked me, but I got her back," Carol replied.

Aunt Connie returned to the kitchen to get started with dinner.

"Oh, so you two were having some fun here. You should have just come to the beach with us if you wanted to soak up the sun and get wet."

"Naw, the salt water fuc—messes up my hair. Oh, hey…" She stopped to take a glance down the hallway to see if her brother was in earshot. "Lynda called today."

"Oh, really? And what did the little bitch have to say?"

"Just wanted to talk to Gary. She's pissed that we moved," Carol said with a beaming smile. "Should I tell him she called?"

Just then, the boys came out of the room, Frank leading the way, but Gary had heard his sister's last remark. "Who's she who called?"

"Lynda did. She called around noon." She went on and told him the whole short conversation.

"Oh, well," was Gary's reply.

"Carol, your big brother is too engrossed in his own hormonal masculinity right now to let Lynda get him down. He got asked out for Saturday night."

"All right, Gary!" Carol yelled. "Who's the lucky victim?"

"He is," Frank jumped in to say. "Karen is hot, she's…" He stopped just in time to realize his mom was within listening distance of their conversation. Just then, she came into the room with dishes for the dining room table.

"Oh, hi, boys. You two have a good time today? How was the first day of practice?"

"Same as always, Mom. They ran our butts off and made us hurt."

"No pain, no gain. That's what your father always told you. Now, Frank, how about you and Gary give me a hand setting the table? Oh, by the way, I talked to your mom today. She's coming by tonight. She said something about a family meeting."

The children's faces fell to a frown. A family meeting? What now?

Their aunt read their grimaces and then added, "She was in a very good mood. She bought a house up here. Oh, my…now I let the surprise out of the bag!"

The kids' attitude instantly changed. They couldn't wait for this meeting tonight.

They finished dinner quickly and stood busy to wait for their mother to arrive with the good news. They all promised their aunt that they would act as surprised as possible. That was going to be hard. It wasn't until seven thirty that evening that their mother arrived. She entered the door to an ambush of what you were to think to be love-starved siblings. After the hugs and kisses were done with, they all sat down to start the "meeting."

"Okay, well, I have some good news for you. I put a down payment on a house today." She stopped to see her children's reaction, which was almost instantaneous. She got the impression real fast that they already knew, and gave her sister a quick smile, which confirmed her suspicions. She went on to tell them about the house. It was only about two miles from their aunt's house and, like their old house, not too far from the beach. It had five bedrooms, three bathrooms, a big family room, and a fenced-in backyard. "I have the closing in two weeks, so we have to start making plans on finishing packing up the old house this week and get ready to move the next weekend." With that, the meeting was adjourned and everyone was all charged with the outcome. The children were all in agreement: the summer stay with their aunt had helped them get acquainted with their new environment. They were eager to make Riverside their new home.

Later that evening, Gary started to think about everything that happened today. In his recall, he was reminded about the fact that Lynda had called. He had mixed feelings about his former girlfriend, but he was reminded about how she treated him. He made up his mind that he would try to meet with her this weekend sometime between packing. He wanted and needed to come to terms with their relationship once and for all. He always held his friends' regard close to his concern, and after all, with Lynda, she surely was the closest friend that he had. He had learned more about himself from her than he could have from anyone else. He also did a lot of the same for her. Perhaps she was right. Maybe it was time to take what they learned from each other and put it to the test. He knew that was going to happen on Saturday night at Barbara's party. He had never kissed another girl other than Lynda. Now there was Karen. He was a little apprehensive about this party. He didn't really know many that were going to be there, so it would be a real initiation to his new classmates. He figured it would be just like entering an online chat room, except no computer and no keyboard. The big difference, though, was he wasn't walking in alone; he would be there with a great-looking girl who asked him to be there with her.

*****

Gary was having this funny feeling hit him. It was like he knew someone was talking about him. He had just gotten out of the shower and was looking forward to lying down to a night of relaxation after his tiring day. What he really needed to unwind was to get online to do some serious chatting. He missed his online friends. Also, he needed something to tire his mind out. His body was wiped, but his mind was still going a mile a minute. He had to settle for a night of television with the family, but even that was nonexistent tonight. Donna was out with Steve. Frank was on the phone with Barbara. Mom, Aunt Connie, and Carol were in the kitchen, chattering away. He plopped down on the couch and started doing some channel surfing. He came upon a rerun episode of *The Wonder Years*. Unfortunately, it was the episode when Kevin broke up with Winnie. He instantly started to think about Lynda again. Yes, he was bitter for what she did, but that didn't change the past that they shared. She was the one thing in his life up to this point that he never could control or ever really wanted to. She challenged him constantly. She pushed him when he wanted to quit. When his mind was stalled, she inspired him to keep thinking. She was just always there for him to try new things with, and he wasn't too afraid to try them as long as she was there. All his inhibitions about his looks, his attitude, and even his own body, she helped him overcome. They shared their new feelings with each other and allowed no queries to go unanswered. They learned a lot about their growing bodies together. From their first kiss to adolescent fondling, they were always in tune with each other's feelings. They had talked about intercourse, but Gary was not sure they should try it. He still had some concerns that they were too young. He had sometimes wondered if his reservations toward having sex were what made her break up with him. She was the impulsive one, where he always thought too much. However, it could have just been their destiny to break so that both could take what they learned from each other and move forward. How hard would it have been to move if she didn't go away for the summer and break up with him? Gary pondered that question but then started to think about his upcoming date with Karen. He had never been out with any other girl except Lynda. How would he measure up? This was a challenge he was eager to engage.

All the pondering along with trying to watch television at the same time had taken its toll on his already-tired body. Gary drifted off to sleep, leaving all his further thoughts of that evening to his dreams.

He arose the next morning to the smell of bacon perusing the household air.

"Hey, look who's finally up!" he heard Carol say.

"About time, bud. You better get up and get moving. We have to be at practice in an hour," Frank added as he grabbed his cousin and rolled him off the couch.

Gary crawled off the floor and straggled into the kitchen. He sat down and was immediately served with a plate consisting of four eggs, six pieces of bacon, four sausage patties, and two pieces of toast.

"What's all this for? I can't eat all this," Gary slurred out, still half-awake.

"You have to. Coach's orders. Frank told me what Coach Parr told you three weeks ago. Can't disagree with him either. You need to put a little meat on those bones, and with me cooking for you, you will. And you should have told me about that three weeks ago too," Aunt Connie said with authority.

Gary was not fully awake yet to battle his aunt. Actually, even if he were fully awake, he might not have been ready. He began to eat his breakfast so he could digest as much of it as possible before practice started.

The second day of practice was even rougher than the first. The coaches were pushing every ounce of sweat out of these would-be athletes. The stress endurance, preparation, and conditioning. Anyone who made this team was going to be ready, or they would be watching from the stands. After the exercises were complete, each coach was introduced and for which squad they were going to be directing. Coach Parr oversaw the defensive backs. He started calling out the list of names and finished off with, "Jim Taylor and Gary Moran." What? Defensive backs? He was going to work out with them? This wasn't right. He was a kicker; what was he doing on defense? He followed the group to one section of the field where the coach started giving his opening speech.

"Okay, men. For you, new guys, let me tell you something about the program we run here. First, we believe in teamwork. Whether you make the varsity or are placed on the JV team, you are all part of the same team here at SCC. We also believe that every member of the team performs for the overall performance of that team, and you will be called forward to fill in at different positions when needed. Our overall scheme has been, a strong defense builds an effective offense. If the other team can't score, they can't win."

They all listened intently to what the coach was saying and prepared themselves mentally for what was to come. Gary particularly paid attention so he could get some idea why he was working with the defense instead of the offense.

"Jimmy, that little guy next to you wants your position this year. Moran, if you want it, you will not only have to outkick him, but you will also have to be able to knock him on his ass." Gary looked at his opponent with disdain. He was looking at a guy ten inches taller than him, with about sixty pounds more in girth. "The kicker on the kickoff team has to work just like a safety. You both have to be able to cut off anything that gets through and take down."

Gary was beginning to understand the reasoning now but was caught off guard by the coach's next question.

"Think you can handle that, Moran?"

Without thinking, he responded quickly, "Bring him on, Coach. I've taken down bigger."

A roar of laugher followed from the other players that had the other groups looking over to see what the commotion was.

"Okay, we will see about that next week, when we get into pads with full contact," Coach Parr answered back to his cockiness. "Right now, let's break out in two groups…"

The boys again began running a new set of drills which worked them harder than they did the day before. Gary's speed was at its best. He stayed up with the receivers and covered the position as well as he could. He started to size up his competition. Where brute power was lacking, intelligence reigned with Gary. He watched Jimmy run. Taking his size, his approximate weight, and how he shifted his balance during standard running maneuvers, he figured where Jimmy's center of gravity was and just where he was going to hit him to take him down next week. Gary's mind was again taking off where his body was at its shortfalls. He knew he probably didn't stand a chance of taking this guy's position this year. Logic dictated that even if he could outkick him, Jimmy was in his senior year. This would be his last year, so he would get the position this year by default, and Gary would just have to be content with the two years after that. Of course, he wasn't just going to sit back and let him have it without putting up some kind of effort. Especially after his big mouth put him in the position to "put up or shut up." He was the new kid, after all. It was apparent that Coach Parr was going to call him out every chance he could, so he looked forward to the challenges that were about to be presented to him.

CHAPTER 6

Saturday morning came upon the Moran family really fast. Aunt Connie had gotten them up very early to make the track back down to their old homestead. Donna was dropped off at the old house the previous night by Steve, so she was already packing with her mom. Gary quickly packed up his computer and other assorted junk he had lying around his room. He worked hard for the first three hours to try to finish as much as he could, so he could get out and meet up with some old friends. He was going out the door to look for Manny when he heard someone scream his name. It was Lynda. Her mother hadn't even stopped the car in the driveway across the street before she had bolted from the vehicle. She ran up to Gary and hugged him furiously, finishing off her embrace with a kiss. Gary kissed her back, but with far less enthusiasm than her. Carol watched the whole display with extreme contempt.

"Wow, I missed kissing you, Gary, and I missed you! Can you take a break so we can talk?"

"Yeah, sure, I think we need to. Carol, tell Mom I'll be back in about a half an hour."

Gary and Lynda walked back across the street. Gary stopped to say hello to Lynda's mother and picked up a couple of bags of groceries from her car to carry in for her.

"Mom, Gary and I are going to talk in my room, okay?"

"Oh, hey, let's go back and sit around the pool," Gary interjected. He wanted to talk, but he didn't want it to be that private. They walked out back, and Gary sat down on a deck chair. "So how was Colorado?"

"Actually, I was only there for two weeks. My dad had some assignments in Arizona, New Mexico, and then we had to fly down to Bolivia for three weeks."

"Wow, well, you really got around this summer. So did you meet any guys in your travels?" Gary said quizzically.

"Yeah, I met a couple. Nothing happened, though. None of them were as great as you are. What about you? You meet anyone up there yet?"

"Yeah, in fact, she invited me to a party tonight." Gary took his shot. She wasn't expecting that.

"So who is she?" she came back with a sly attitude.

"Just a girl that I met after practice. She's a cheerleader and a friend of Frank's girlfriend."

"A cheerleader! You're going out with a cheerleader? I thought they weren't your type."

"I'm not really sure what my type is. And besides, she asked me out, so I guess I'm her type," Gary retorted in his defense.

"So I guess you are moving on…away from me."

"Well, that was your idea, wasn't it? What did you think, we just pick up again now when you got back? Sorry, I don't think that's going to work for me."

"But I thought you loved me?" She started to cry softly but could not hold it all back. Gary moved nearer to her and pulled her into his shoulder and held her instinctively to calm her tears. It wasn't fair. Crying was a hard weapon to deal with, but he did his share of crying, so he had to bear down and maintain control here today.

"I do love you. The things we did together. The good times we had. You will always be special to me, but I gave it a lot of thought this summer on us breaking up and being apart, and now we are apart. You were right for breaking up."

"You just have that new girlfriend you're going out with there already!" Her mood changed as she stopped crying and pushed him away.

"She's not my girlfriend. I just met her Tuesday, and she asked me to go to her friend's party tonight. It's just a date. But what about you? How many guys did you meet over the summer?" Gary wasn't about to lose this battle. "Did you come back with your virginity still intact?" That was mean, but he had to do it. Besides, deep down he really wanted to know.

"Yeah, I did. I came close to doing it with this guy I met in Arizona, but I stopped because I wanted my first time to be with you. Damn, was I stupid!"

"Oh, so you whored around while you were away, and there you stand and criticize me for just getting a date on a Saturday night?" He backed farther away from her. He knew things were about to get nasty.

"Fuck you, you bastard! Get the fuck out of here!" She rushed at him and started to push him back toward the porch door.

"So much for talking, huh? So fine, I'm gone, you little bitch… and don't call me anymore on the phone or online." He had turned to walk out the door when she ran and jumped on his back, reaching around and scratching his neck. He reacted quickly and moved to get her off him and rotated around to fend off her sudden attack. She jumped at him again, but this time he was ready for her. He tried to calm her down, but to no avail. He wasn't the type to hit girls, especially Lynda, no matter how angry he was. She continued to swing at him and screaming obscenities. Finally, Gary had enough, and he had to do something. When she lunged again, he grabbed her arm and pulled her to him. He quickly reached behind her head and pulled it toward his own. He kissed her squarely on the lips, which stopped her rage for a moment. He then reached down with his other arm and brought it around her legs and lifted her right off the ground. Still kissing her, he moved over the edge of the pool and dropped her in, clothes and all.

"That should cool you off! Now, listen to me. I don't want to be enemies here, so don't push the issue. You closed the door in our relationship, and it opened others for the both of us, separately. Deal with it. I'm going now. I have to finish packing." He turned and started out the door. As he walked away, he heard a faint cry.

"Bye, Gary."

He walked back across the street, where he was greeted by his sister Carol.

"Hey, what the hell happened to your neck? Did she scratch you or something? You're bleeding!" Carol said as he approached.

He reached up to his neck and felt his wound. He hadn't noticed any pain until that very moment that his sister pointed out the fact that he was bleeding. "Yeah, I guess she got me." Just then, their mom and sister came out of the house carrying boxes and ran over to Gary, who now had blood all over his neck, hands, and shirt. He was explaining to his mother what happened when Lynda's mom walked up and was quite surprised at Gary's condition.

"Did Lynda do that to you?" Gary nodded. "I'm so sorry she did that…"

"It's no big deal, Mary. He'll live," Gary's mom said. "It's already starting to clot."

"Well, I guess that explains why Lynda came in and ran into the bathroom soaking wet and crying. She said you threw her in the pool. That's all I was able to get out of her behind the locked door. What happened?"

"We just had an argument, that's all. She went ballistic and started hitting me and scratching me. I couldn't get her to stop. I didn't want to hit her, so I picked her up and threw her in the pool."

"Well, then, she deserved what she got, then," Mary said with a firm smile. Carol had brought out the first aid supplies and was listening to Gary's description of the confrontation.

"Ya should have decked her, Gar!" Carol remarked, getting into the conversation.

"Carol!" her mom said. "Stop that talk now. Your brother is too much of a gentleman to hit a girl…there, the bleeding stopped already."

"Oh, that battle scar's gonna look really cute on your date tonight, bro," Donna added with a small laugh.

He didn't give that a thought until then. Now he had to go in and see just how bad the scratch was, so he could deal with the paranoia until tonight. He left the girls to go inside to do his own doctoring of his "battle scar."

The rest of the afternoon went on uneventful. They made the trip back to their aunt's house in time for Gary and Frank to get cleaned up and ready for the party. It took a little begging, but he was able to talk Donna into driving them to pick up Karen in lieu of Aunt Connie.

Gary approached the door with some hesitation. The verbal coaching from his sister and cousin, who were waiting in the car, was not helping him vent his nervousness. He had never had to pick up a date at her house and meet the girl's parents for the first time. But he finally knocked on the door and prayed for Karen to answer it. The door opened abruptly, and there stood Karen. His heart started to beat once more.

"Hi, Gary. Come on in. My parents want to meet you," she said with a smile.

"Hi, Karen, sure…"

Karen opened the door wider to allow him to enter.

"Mom, Gary's here," she announced as she closed the door behind him. He walked into the living room, and a man close to twice his size stood up and extended his hand.

"Hey, there, Gary. Name's Jim Taylor. Nice to meet you," he said as he shook his hand with a strong grip.

"Hi, Mr. Taylor. Nice to meet you too."

"I heard you just moved up here to go to SCC, and you are all ready to play some football to boot."

"Well, I'm going to try, sir. They got a tough program going here. I'm just looking to fit in and play as part of the team."

"That's good. We can use some more guys with your attitude on the team. I heard the coach rides you a lot."

"A little, but I got a lot of that last year, too, when I went out for football for the first time at my old school."

"You think you are good enough to make the varsity squad? What are you trying out for again…kicker, right?"

"Yes, that's right. I'm trying out for placekicker. I hope to make the team." He was getting a little puzzled about everything this guy knew about him. He didn't know Karen knew that much about him. "You seem to have heard a lot about me, sir. I feel I'm at a disadvantage here." He looked at Karen. What, was she checking up on him on the field?

Just then, the front door opened and in walked a too familiar face. It was his opposition for the kicker position this year, Jimmy. He never connected the name to just then. Now he knew where Karen's father was coming from. He had to think fast to stay ahead of what might come.

"Oh, Gary, you already know my brother, don't you?"

"Hi, Jimmy. I did not know that Karen was your sister. Small world?"

"You should know, a small world is what you live in," Jimmy replied with a sly smile. "Didn't know you liked going out with underclassmen, Karen?"

"Jimmy! Be nice now. He's a guest here," Karen's mom said as she entered the room.

Finally, some relief, Gary thought to himself.

"Hello, Mrs. Taylor," Gary responded quickly to change the flow of the conversation. "Thanks. You walked in right on time. I was a little outnumbered here."

"Hi, Gary, don't let these two bully you. You weren't in any trouble. Karen knows how to handle the men in this family. I'm sure she wouldn't have let you get hurt."

"Yeah, besides, I can't wait until I watch you put this guy on his butt next week," Karen said as she playfully pushed her brother back as she moved next to Gary. "We really got to get going. I'll be home by ten, okay?"

"Oh, that's right, Donna and Frank are waiting in the car, and my sister doesn't like to wait."

"Okay, get going, then. Ten is fine. Don't keep me up waiting. Have fun! And, Gary, I'm sure you are going to fit in just fine here," Mr. Taylor said as he put a firm grip on his shoulder. They then both said their goodbyes and were out the door. They climbed into the back seat, Gary made a quick introduction of Karen to Donna, and they were on their way.

"You handled yourself pretty good in there. I think my father was impressed."

"God, I hope so. If I ever piss you off, give me a chance to apologize before telling him anything. Donna, the guy was huge. He put his hand on my shoulder, and I thought he was going to snap my collarbone from the weight."

"Don't worry, you're safe with me. I fight my own battles, and I don't take prisoners." She gave him a light punch in the arm to make her point. She moved closer to him and bent over to whisper in his ear, "So you remember that and stay by me the rest of the evening with that charm of yours and I might let you live to enjoy the evening." She then just gave him a quick kiss on the cheek, which left him with a small smile on his blushed face.

They arrived at the party around seven o'clock. The music was blaring, and there were people dancing and talking all around. Frank had quickly found Barbara in the crowd. Gary saw a lot of guys there were on the football team. He moved around the crowd meeting his new classmates, and Karen was almost always by his side. He danced a few songs with her, and on the one slow song, she cuddled close to him as he held her in his arms. She was great to be with. She laughed at all his jokes, talked intelligently, and was one of the most beautiful girls in the room. He found out that she was fifteen years old, which surprised him, because she was as tall as he was and thought she was younger. She was in fact a sophomore also, and both her parents were alumni of SCC. Her brother had already had college scouts looking at him and looked like he was destined to be attending a top university next year with scholarship. This confirmed his speculations of him not making varsity this year.

After some time, the music was shut off and someone announced, "Karaoke!" For the next forty-five minutes, the party was aroused by the talents of some would-be entertainers. He found out that the school had a very big performing arts program, of which Barbara and a lot of her friends were part. Barbara was acting as emcee as she moved around the room, coaxing her friends to get up and sing. Some were very good, while others were totally comical.

Gary was somewhat uneasy as he saw her looking in his direction.

"Gary Moran! Come on, Gary, get up here and let's hear ya!" she boomed over the speakers.

With a little encouragement from Karen, he approached the microphone. He did not get to choose his song. They were playing

"Kamikaze Karaoke," so Karen reached into the bowl and pulled out the name of the song he had to sing. It was "I Will Do Anything for Love" by Meatloaf. Okay, this wasn't going to be too bad; he knew the song. The music started, and the words came up on the screen and he began to sing. He was a young man with many talents, but singing wasn't one of his better ones. He decided to take Karen's earlier advice and looked right at her during the whole song and sang it directly to her. She even was prompted to jump in and sing the female part of the finale of the song. At its conclusion, the two, standing together, moved closer to each other and, as befitting the song, embraced and kissed in front of the whole crowd. After the applause and the "Ahhs" died down, they both went outside for some fresh air. He was quite proud of himself with that feat, but he knew he wouldn't have been able to do it without Karen. And the kiss—now that was a load off his mind on getting by that icebreaker. His first kiss after Lynda, and he did it in front of everyone.

There were more kisses to follow that evening. With every kiss, a new memory was created, blocking out the confrontation of the earlier afternoon.

After dropping her off at the house, he was wild with anticipation of the upcoming year at his new home, his new school, and his new life. His father was right in his planning of his future, and he was right in trusting in it.

CHAPTER 7

He unlocked the door at the new office and entered cautiously. As he looked around, it was apparent that all the furniture and equipment were set up and ready for them to begin their next operation. Miguel walked out from the back room carrying another monitor and set in on the rear desk to hook it up.

"Hey, boss, didn't hear you come in. Did you enjoy your vacation?"

Jerry was still looking around and was in deep thought and didn't answer him right away. "Yeah, everything was good. How many connections do we have to work with in this building?"

"I'm reading twenty-four totals. I already was able to hack into four, but give me a couple more days and I should be able to access at least twelve to fourteen. Do we have the target picked out yet?"

"Well, we did, but as of three weeks ago, Lauren told me he moved. We had a possible of three targets in the South Florida area, so we might have to push back our schedule a bit, but I think we'd be fine with whichever way we go. Have you seen Lauren yet today?"

"Yeah, she told me you were coming in today, so she went out to bring back lunch for us. She's been chatting up a storm for the last three days. She makes a really good teenage girl."

"She should. She's only twenty-two. Let's hope she made some progress with tracking down our primary target."

Jerry sat down at the center desk and started to review the stack of files waiting for him. He didn't like Miami. The humidity was hell, and the heat was more than he wanted to deal with. He did his time back when he was in the Marines in his early twenties. Now at forty-five, he wanted nothing to do with it. That was the reason he moved to Boston after his discharge, to be part of law enforcement.

He didn't really like that, but after the Marines, he didn't really have a place to go. Becoming a policeman was an easy hire for him. He had spent eight years on the street and finally got promoted to detective. He only did it for the pay raise. Law enforcement didn't really satisfy his money requirements. He was driven to make more money so he could travel and enjoy life, but by the time he hit forty, he just wasn't seeing that happen. He was moved to the internet crime section of the department and even had assignments with the FBI federal task force. On this one case, a pedophile went online and met a twelve-year-old girl he was able to coerce into meeting him. He abducted her and later killed her. He was a true amateur and was easily tracked down by the police following the IP connection that he used to contact the girl online. Jerry studied the case and learned from this guy's mistakes. Jerry was no pedophile. He wasn't driven by a sick mind whose desires treaded over caution. He didn't want to kill anyone either. He wanted money, and lots of it. It was two years since he put together this team of four to do just that. In that time, he had successfully abducted six boys aged thirteen to seventeen, collected over fifteen million dollars in ransom, and then released his abductees safely with no harm. He knew the federal task force was investigating the abductions, but he knew how they worked. He knew, being patient and cautious, he could do about two more jobs and then retire untouched. He researched his targets as to their vulnerabilities, their patterns, and their state of mind, and of course, their family's wealth. He stayed away from females; they were too protected in today's society. Children who were under twelve also brought out public sentiment when news of abduction was announced. But teenage boys were easy prey when you used the right bait. A boy who had to deal with a deep emotional loss or drastic change in his personal life was open to approach. Add to that raging hormones and an opportunity to meet a cute teenage girl online and their target made the list. He was aware of all the online traps because he was on that side of the fence once. His targets were found, investigated, and verified before they even made the list. Their family's ability to pay a ransom and how much was also verified and taken into account. It was a lot of investigative work, much like he did as a detective, but with a much better pay scale.

Lauren walked through the door carrying a bag of sandwiches from a local Cuban café, followed by Eddie carrying a carrier with four drinks. The whole team had finally arrived to start the next operation. Jerry was the brains, Miguel was the tech, Eddie was the muscle, and Lauren was the bait. They all sat quietly and ate while Jerry continued reading the files during lunch.

Jerry was the first to speak, and like it was a military operation, he quickly started to fire off questions for his troops to respond.

"Miguel already told me where he is with the computer setup. Eddie, did you make it out to the island to see if it's still a viable holding site?"

"Yes, and it's still untouched. No one goes there. I have to go back out and repair the wall of the hut to secure it if we are going to use it. There's a lot of wildlife out there, so it's not too safe in the condition it's in right now."

"All right, let's get it fixed. We have three possible targets, so we will assume right now that we are going to use it. Lauren, baby, you're up. How you making out with our boys?"

"Well, I found our primary target. I went to church last Sunday and found him sitting with the family. I got talking to this couple whose son goes to the same school. I didn't meet the son, so before you get all uptight, don't! He plays football and is in the same grade, so there was a possibility that he knows our target. I found the boy last night and am going to run into him again tonight."

"I don't know. This seems like it's going to take some time to make a connection again with our target. What about the other two?"

"Well, the one from Hollywood is not talking to me right now. We are having a fight." Lauren smiled at the sound of her online tiff with a perfect stranger. Jerry was not amused. "The one from Miami Beach wants to meet me in a real bad way."

"I have been giving this a thought. I think we are only going to do two more projects and quit for a while. Eddie, do we have a secondary holding area that we can mobilize and use if we needed to?"

"Yeah, I have two possible locations. One is more readily prepared than the island. What do you have in mind?" Eddie answered.

"I talked to a detective on the task force last week. We were shooting the shit, and he told me about the ongoing investigations on these serial abduction cases. They have our MO as hitting, waiting, and moving between cases. I'm thinking we take the Miami Beach target first, complete it, and then wait, but this time, we don't move out of Miami. We stay here and get jobs and blend in for a couple of months. The task force will assume we moved to a new location, so we use that time to re-establish our primary, then take him down. Miami Beach is an estimated six million, and Palm Beach is another eight. That will get us over thirty-six million. We split it up and disappear."

The team sat there and absorbed Jerry's plan. This was a definite change in the way they worked, but the idea had enough merit to further discuss it. They spent the rest of the day going over the files to keep in preparation of whatever they decided. The team as a whole had no weak link when it came to intelligence. Even Lauren, at her young age, was a seasoned manipulator. They got this far on being and doing the smart thing. They had been smarter than the local police, smarter than the task force, and smarter than their targets. Nothing was going to change that now.

CHAPTER 8

Monday morning finally arrived, and the coaches started passing out the pads, helmets, and practice uniforms. Gary was given his old number, 11. He guessed the coach really did remember him from the game last year. He proudly put on his practice jersey over his pads to check out its fit. It was official to him; he was now an SCC Wildcat. He finished getting dressed and started going out to the field.

"Hey, Moran, wait up!" someone called from behind him. "I have a message for you," he said as he caught up to him. Gary knew his name was Mike, but really didn't know him more from most of the guys on the team. "Do you go by the screen name *Pkicker* online?" he blurted out while he caught his breath.

"Yeah, I do. Who is the message from?"

"I've been talking to these girls online who say they know you, Lisa and Kim. Do you know them?"

"Yeah, I've talked to them, mostly Kim, but I haven't been online for almost a month, so it's been a while. How did they know you knew me?"

"I've been talking to Lisa about two weeks, and we were talking about schools we go to, and then her friend Kim joined the conversation last night and asked how many Catholic schools were there in Palm Beach around Riverside. It was weird. She described you pretty good. I thought you moved from Miami, not Vermont?"

"I did. I've never been to Vermont and haven't even met Kim or Lisa in real life. How did they describe me?"

"She just said if I knew a small brainy kid who's a kicker on the football team with a smart-ass attitude. You had to be the guy."

Gary chuckled at his description. He wondered if that really was the reputation he was going to have to live down.

"So what is the message?"

"Just say hi and ask you when you are going to be online again."

"I'm getting my computer hooked up this weekend, so she will have to wait till then."

"Why wait? Are you doing anything tonight? You can come over for dinner and use mine. Do you like Italian? My mom is a great cook."

"I'd have to clear it with my aunt, but sure, thanks. Hey, we better get out to the field. I want to loosen up a bit and get used to the added weight. I have to be able to tackle someone today."

"Yeah, Jimmy, I know."

"You do? How…"

"The whole team knows that you said you were going to knock him on his ass. Man, I hope you can do it. This ought to be good."

"I didn't say I was going to knock him on his ass. I just said I was going to tackle him."

"Same thing. Whoa…look at that."

They both stopped in their tracks as they turned the corner. The stands were full of onlookers. As they approached the field, the crowd erupted in applause. *Funny,* Gary thought, *I didn't think the Romans cheered the Christians right before they were thrown to the lions.* In Gary's case, though, it was a wildcat that he had to go up against.

As he scanned the crowd, he saw Karen's dad. Karen was on the sidelines with all the other cheerleaders. Just then, he heard his own name being yelled and saw his sisters and Steve walking up into the stands. He couldn't believe it. His own family knew about this and didn't warn him. He ran out to the field and started to stretch and loosen up. Then it occurred to him: if he was going to get some respect from this, he thought he would try to impress the crowd before he made a complete fool out of himself. He turned to Mike and told him of his idea. Mike ran to get some footballs and encouraged the aid of another player.

The coaches were starting to make their way to the field. Gary walked over to Karen, took off his helmet, and dropped it to the ground. He put his arms around her and gave her the most romantic kiss he had ever given. It was long, wet, and with a lot of tongue.

The crowd became silent. Without saying a word to her, he then picked up his helmet and ran back to the field. He ran to the 25-yard line, where Mike and another player were waiting. Gary pointed with his foot to a spot on the field and then walked backward, pacing off his steps. Mike knelt down on one knee and yelled, "Hike!" The ball was shuttled back to Mike's waiting hands, and he placed it down on the turf. Gary's foot connected with the ball at a split second after it was placed down. The ball sailed up and through the uprights. The crowd cheered. A 35-yard field goal! They moved back five yards and repeated the routine. Again, the ball sailed through the goalposts. A 40-yard field goal. Moving back another five yards, he again kicked the ball with the same results. A 45-yard field goal. The crowd in the stands was on their feet with a roar. They moved back another five feet. Gary had never completed anything longer than what he had just accomplished, and never in a game situation, but he wasn't going to stop now. The adrenaline was pumping. He had a crowd of people who came there to see what he was made of, and a quitter at that point just wasn't it. The crowd became silent, as if an actual game were taking place. The ball was hiked, Mike set it down, and Gary kicked it. It was up. It was going. It was going. It started to pull to the right with a strong breeze coming from the left. Bam! It hit the upright and fell to the ground. The "Ohhs" and "Ahhs" were very prevalent at that point, but then a surprising thing happened. Karen's dad stood up and started to applaud his effort. Soon the entire crowd was on its feet, clapping and yelling, "GAR-REE! GAR-REE!" They walked back to the other players, who were on the sidelines with the coaches, waiting for the entertainment to end.

"Okay, let's get this practice going before *The Moran Show* gets picked up by ESPN," Coach Lewis said. Almost everyone laughed. Everyone, that is, except Gary. He was not going to let anything take away from his concentration right now. Not even any of the coach's remarks were going to interfere with Gary's building aggression. This "show" wasn't over yet. He was pumped, and he was determined that he was going to stay that way all the way through practice, until he had to unload on Jimmy.

He went through all the drills without saying a word. Even when Coach Parr walked by and said, "Nice kicking there, Gary," he didn't acknowledge him. He just continued with his performance.

Then came the tackling drill. This was what everyone came to see.

"Okay, let's get this over with. Taylor, on your back. You are the runner." He tossed the ball to him, and he lay on his back on the field. "Okay, Moran, it's time. Let's get this show going so we can get on to some serious practicing."

Gary didn't say a word or make any gesture of response. He lay on his back, facing the other direction, ten feet from Jimmy's position. The whistle blew, and the two were up on their feet and raced toward each other. Gary moved out of a direct line from his attacker and came at him at a slight angle. He crouched down and came in low into Jimmy's right side just as he was planting his left foot. Gary's shoulder hit below Jimmy's rib cage, below the protection of his shoulder pads. He wrapped his right hand around his midsection and moved the left down and around the right leg of his opponent. The sudden impact on Jimmy's torso immediately knocked the wind out of him and slowed his momentum down. With all the weight on Jimmy's left leg, Gary only had to pick up on the right leg to take him off balance. Gary's legs did everything else as he kept his momentum going and rode Jimmy to the ground. He got up as fast as he could even though the tackle had exhausted him. Jimmy didn't get up at all. He had to get his air back first. Gary stood there and reached down to give him a hand getting to his feet. Jimmy stood there and looked down at the runt who just knocked him silly. He smiled and held his hand out to Gary. They shook hands to the cheering of the crowd.

"Well, you swept Karen off her feet with that kiss, and now you knocked me off my feet with that tackle. What's next? You ready to take on my dad?" Jimmy said laughingly.

"Fuck that! Stop! You can have the position!" Gary responded with a small smile while backing away. "I'd rather go out for the band than tackle with your dad."

"Well, we can agree on something there…think how it's been growing up with him."

"Okay, okay, let's get back to business here!" Coach Lewis barked.

The team continued with the practice as the stands started to slowly empty. Jimmy and Gary spent a good part of the rest of practice on their kicking game. Gary learned a couple of things from him. They both came through the ordeal rather well and became friends by the end of practice.

It was around two o'clock when the boys got home from practice. Gary remembered about how his sisters knew about the impending show earlier in the day and started to remember that he should be angry with them for the unshared knowledge. He stormed into the house, slamming the door behind him and throwing down his gym bag. He made a beeline for their bedroom.

"Why didn't you tell me I was going to be walking into some freak show this morning?"

"Didn't think you needed to know," Donna responded.

"I didn't need to know? Thanks a lot. The coach has been on my ass since I've been here, and I'm trying like hell to get by his bullshit and you don't think I need to know when I might be walking into a situation that I could be totally embarrassed?"

"Hey, it's not like you didn't come through out there or anything. We knew you could handle it, Gar," Carol said, "and besides, we were there to cheer you on, not make fun of you. Not like you needed any cheering after that kiss you gave that cheerleader."

"Yeah, well, it still would have been nice to have some warning."

"Oh, bull, you know you got off on all that today. I'm betting that you probably were the one to spread the word, so you would have a big audience to pull it on. Didn't ya?" Donna came back defensively.

"No, I didn't. I don't know enough people here to pull something like that off...yet?" He started to loosen up and grin. She was right. If he had thought of it, he might have devised something like that. Unfortunately, this time he was caught completely off guard. He was rather proud of his accomplishments of the morning, though. He really enjoyed the challenge of having to improvise at a moment's notice.

He left the girls to themselves and went to find his aunt to talk her into taking him over to Mike's house. They already had it worked out with Mike's mom, who came to pick him up after practice, that he was invited over for dinner that evening. He was, of course, successful with his aunt.

Mike Mazza was fourteen years old and was just entering SCC also for the first time, but as a freshman. Born in New York City and a son of Italian immigrants, he had lived here for five years. He was a couple of inches taller than Gary, but much more muscular. He was a good-looking boy with an attitude prevalent among the streetwise kids of the Bensonhurst area of Brooklyn. Mike and Gary were alike in a lot of ways. Mike also had a high IQ, although his hormonal growth spurts had started earlier than Gary's. He grew up in a tough neighborhood earlier in his life, like Gary; however, living in Lake Worth, Florida, for the last five years was a big difference from living in New York. He was someone Gary could relate to. He had to adjust at one point to moving to a new city, just like Gary was doing now. They were the perfect friends for each other at a very trying time in their young lives. They were destined to take on their new school together.

Gary arrived promptly at five o'clock. After he had met Mike's parents and two younger brothers, they all sat down to a home-cooked Italian dinner consisting of spaghetti with meat sauce, meatballs, sausage, and salad. The smell of the simmering tomatoes, garlic, onions, and basil was like he was used to with his mom's and aunt's cooking. Mike's mom dished out a big helping of spaghetti for Gary.

"Here, Gary, you eatta this all. Itta make-a big and strong so those bigga guys don't hurta you on the football field."

"Grazie, Signora Mazza, osserva e sente l'odore de grande," Gary replied. It smells and looks great, in Italian.

"Ahh, you speaka Italiano?" Mike's dad said.

"Only a little. My grandfather taught me some words when I was younger. I'm half-Italian on my mother's side. My grandparents are from Sicily."

"Ah, you sucha nice-a boy, now eat! Munga!"

The dinner continued with varied conversation between each other's family history. It was like having family dinner at his grandparents' house. He was very comfortable with them.

After dinner was over, Mike and Gary exited to the living room, where the computer was set up. Finally, after two months without any online chatting, Gary was looking forward to this. First, Mike signed on under his screen name to see if Lisa or Kim was online. They weren't. He signed out and allowed Gary to sign in under a guest account. Gary went to his email account and saw that he had twenty-three emails waiting for him there. He quickly scanned the list and found that ten were just advertising, twelve were from Lynda, and one from Kim. He deleted the ads without reading them and skipped on looking at the letters from his former girlfriend. Kim's email was nothing except that she loved the poem and for him to hurry back as soon as he got his computer hooked back up. He quickly wrote her a quick email back to say hi and told her that he was at a friend's house, using his computer to check his mail and write this letter. He opted to hold back the fact that the friend's computer that he was on was Mike's. He figured he'd have a little fun with her later if she was to come online. He signed off and let Mike back in to sign back on. They spent the next hour chatting in various chat rooms and talking to each other during the interim to get to know each other better.

It was about seven thirty that Lisa got online and messaged them. Mike talked to her briefly, not letting on that Gary was there with him. Just then, she told him that Kim had just signed on and wanted to talk to him. She sent an invitation to both to go into a private room, so they could all talk at the same time.

> **LissieQT:** *Hey, Mike, how was the first day of practice with full pads?*
> **MazmanFL:** *Rough and hot but I survived to be here to talk to you.*
> **LissieQT:** *Yeah, right! For me? You survived? I feel so lucky!*

MazmanFL: No, I'm the lucky one. I'm in here with not one but two fine looking girls. I'm not worthy!! LOL

Chickee89: Oh, God, You're right. You're not!! LOL

LissieQT: We'll see how worthy you are in December; I might be going with Kim to Florida.

Chickee89: Yeah, then we will be checking you out to see if you are anything like you described yourself as. Why don't you have a pic?

MazmanFL: I'm working on it. You won't be disappointed.

Chickee89: So, hey did you find Gary down there yet. Was that kicker out there him?

The boys quickly changed places, allowing Gary access to the keyboard. Now it was time for some fun.

MazmanFL: Yeah, it was him but are you sure you want to meet him?

Chickeee89: Why? What's wrong with him? Did you talk to him?

LissieQT: Why do you say that?

MazmanFL: Because he's short and ugly, that's why.

Chickee89: No, he's not. Gary is cute; I have a pic of him. Are you sure you got the right guy?

LissieQT: He is short, but he is not ugly at all.

MazmanFL: Yep, same guy and what an asshole! You sure you want to meet him when you come down here.

Chickee89: He's not an asshole but I'm starting to think you are.

LissieQT: Mike, not nice, I'm not sure we want to meet you when we come down there.

MazmanFL: Oh, you will meet me…you will meet both of us.

Chickee89: Both? Who's there with you?

65

MazmanFL: Only the ugliest guy in Riverside. It's me, Kim, Gary.

Chickee89: *Gary Moran, you are an ASSHOLE!! Lol*

Chickee89: *Actually, both of you are assholes for putting us through all that.*

LissieQT: *Is Mike still there or has it been you all along?*

MazmanFL: He's been here the whole time. He invited me over for dinner and internet. He was talking to you at first and then I jumped in.

LissieQT: *Oh, so you were both in on this shit.*

MazmanFL: No, don't get mad at Mike, this was all my idea. After all I was just fulfilling your description of me as a "short brainy guy with a smart-ass attitude"

Chickee89: *Oh, sorry, Mike wasn't supposed to tell you that.*

MazmanFL: You get what you ask for. Still want to meet me? Lol

Chickee89: *Oh, yeah, more than ever…just to come down there and beat you up a bit. LOL*

MazmanFL: Get in line. I will have to tell you a about my run in with Lynda this weekend.

Chickee89: *What happened?*

MazmanFL: Too long to tell you now. You will have to wait for this weekend. We move into our new house and my computer will be up and running by then.

Just then, there was a horn honking out in front of the house. Gary looked at his watch and saw that it was eight o'clock and that must be his aunt there to pick him up.

MazmanFL: Got to go. My aunt is here. Here's Mike back. Get him to tell you what happened at practice today. Bye Kim, Bye Lisa.

Chickee89: _Bye Gary_
LissieQT: _Bye-bye Gary_

Gary said good night to his new friend and the rest of the Mazza family and left. He was surprised as his sister was waiting with a stern look on her face.

"I hope this guy isn't going to be a real good friend. He lives way too far away for me to be crating your ass back and forth like this," she remarked as he climbed into the front seat. She was in one of her atypical bitchy moods. Gary had to deal with it as usual and just keep his mouth shut. Sometimes he got into the challenging mode and tried to counter, and sometimes he would come out ahead. The dangerous part was that his sister was just as formidable in a challenge of wits as he was. One that he had come to rely on as an ally, not a foe. There was something wrong, though. He decided that it was going to be his turn to become the sibling shoulder to turn to. After about ten minutes into the ride home, he felt safe enough to say something to get a conversation going.

"So what happened to Aunt Connie? How come she didn't come and pick me up tonight?"

"She volunteered me. Do you know it takes twenty minutes each way to this Mike's house?"

"I do now. Sorry, sis, I didn't know he lived that far away. But hey, he has internet, so this weekend, once I am back online, I can talk to him online, and that should minimize the traveling."

"Or you can have his big brother or big sister drive him and you back and forth when you want to do your male bonding shit."

"Oh, sorry, sis. He's the eldest. He only has two younger brothers. He's not as lucky as I am to have an older sister like you."

"Ass-kisser!" she said, finally breaking a smile. "Well, it's okay. Just let's not make this a regular thing, okay?"

"Yeah, yeah, no problem." He finally got her to lighten up a bit, but he could tell there was still something bothering her. He got her talking, so he wasn't going to stop now. "Hey, Donna, is something wrong? You seem a little out of it tonight."

"Nothing you can help me with, Gar. It's between me and Steve. It's out of your league, kiddo."

"Out of my league? Come on. What could possibly be out of my league? You know we can talk about anything."

"Trust me, we may talk about a lot of things, but I don't think I will ever be discussing my sex life with you."

"Try me. And what could be wrong with your sex life, anyway? You and Steve are great together in public. So how can you two be having problems with sex."

"You see? You just proved my point. You don't know anything about sex in a relationship. I can't believe I'm even having this conversation with you."

"You have been going out with Steve for three years now. What happened now that suddenly you are having problems having sex after all that time?"

"Oh, little brother, are you really lost? What makes you think we have been having sex for all that time?"

"You haven't? I thought…"

"You thought wrong. Sometimes you think too much. Sex is not something you can just pick up from some book, like you always like to do. For your information, bro, I'm still a virgin. Stir that little bit of 411 in your brain and see what you come up with."

"Oh…sorry, Donna, I didn't know. I just assumed…"

"Yes, you did. Don't worry about me, Gar. I'm still holding out. You aren't the only one who must try to live by Daddy's ideals and dreams. That's the problem. It's getting harder not to, now that Steve and I are apart so much. I'm afraid that if we don't do it, we will move further away from each other."

"Wow, sis, you're right. I don't really know what to say, but whatever you decide, I'm sure it would be the right thing."

"Hey, wait a minute, what about you? I know you are still a virgin, but how long is that going to last now that you are dating a fifteen-year-old?"

"What? You mean Karen? Well, we aren't really dating or anything. I just went out with her once."

"Been meaning to ask how that works. You're fourteen, she's fifteen. What's the attraction? Ever think about that one, brainiac?"

"First of all, she doesn't look fifteen. Second, age doesn't matter as long as we have something in common."

"Like what? Your hands on those tits of hers? Better watch out, Gar. There's something more going on with that girl. You might just be one of her conquests."

"She's not like that!" Gary said defensively.

"Oh, and how do you know that? You tried to run a hand into that shirt and she pushed you away?"

"Yeah, exactly. I thought you didn't want to talk about sex with me."

"No, I said I wasn't going to discuss *my* sex life. I didn't say we couldn't talk about yours." Donna was having some fun now. Gary's attempt to cheer her up had backfired on him. "You virgin males are so temperamental."

"Hey, wait a minute. How do you know I'm still a virgin, anyway?"

"Think about it, bro. The only girl you have ever been that close with was Lynda, and that horny little thing liked to brag to Carol on everything you two used to do with each other. And Carol tells me everything. If you had fucked her, we would have known about it."

"She told Carol what we used to do...what we did..." Gary was flustered now. Not a very common sight, but Donna was enjoying it. "Damn, that little bitch. I should have decked her the other day."

"Oh, stop! You know you wouldn't do that. Besides, the way I heard it, you were pretty good at making a girl feel good. You taught Carol more about sex than I was told at her age."

"I didn't teach her anything. You really think I would tell her about sex? She's getting your body, and that's hard enough to deal with without giving her any other ideas."

"Well, you didn't teach her directly. You taught Lynda, and she passed it on to your little sister. But the big question is, Where did you learn it?"

"Books, remember?" He had realized that he was getting a little agitated and thought he better calm down a bit and start changing the subject. When he was younger, he used to have a quick temper, but his dad worked hard at getting him to control it. He used what his dad taught him earlier in the day, how to turn his anger into a positive force.

It was at that moment that they pulled into their aunt's driveway. They got out of the car, and Gary stopped and looked at the starlit sky.

"Donna? Do you remember what Dad looked like? I mean… without looking at a picture."

"Sometimes I do, but sometimes it's like I can't remember him at all. Do you?"

"Yeah, most of the time, depending where I'm at. Do you remember a long time ago, when we were at the beach and Dad borrowed that surfboard and went out and took some waves?"

"You remember that? You were only about seven when he did that."

"Yeah, I do. Every time I go surfing with Steve and get on the board, I see Dad in my mind doing it. And the time we used to go up on the roof and lie down and look up at the stars and talk. Usually on nights just like this, so quiet…and peaceful…" His words drifted off into silence.

His thoughts of his father had started to take their toll. He walked over to a patch of grass and sat down and started to cry softly. Donna sat down next to him and put her arm around her little brother. She, too, had teary eyes, and all of a sudden, her problems with her relationship with Steve were distant at that moment.

"I miss him too, Gary. He wanted so much to see us grow up. Especially you. He would have been very proud of you for what you did today. You know, he'd have been in those stands with us, watching you knock the shit out of that guy."

Gary rubbed his eyes and pressed out a smile at his sister's remark. He probably would have been there. He looked up into the sky and stared intently at the stars above. "I think he was there. Sometimes I think he's always up there, looking down on us."

"Let's go in. I think I need to call Steve."

"Whatcha going to tell him?"

"That I love him. That should hold him for a while. And I love you too, you horny little virgin." She squeezed him tightly while she said that last line and finished off with a kiss on his cheek. She stood up and reached her hand down to Gary to help him up. "Well, you coming?"

"Not yet. I'm going to stay out here a bit."

She turned and started to walk into the house, but as usual, Gary always wanted to get the last snide remark in.

"Oh, hey, Donna?"

She stopped and turned back with a glare of anticipation of what he was about to say.

"When I lose my virginity, I'll tell you about it first before Carol, okay?"

"Yeah, thanks. I guess that would be better than hearing it from our darling little sister. Don't stay out here too late. You have practice in the morning. Oh, and, Gary, if you want to remember what Dad looks like, look in a mirror." She turned and walked into the house.

He stayed there for about ten minutes, thinking about his dad. After he was confident that his red eyes had cleared, removing the fact that he had been crying, he went inside and went to bed.

CHAPTER 9

Saturday came up fast, and it was a busy day for all the Moran family and friends. Jimmy and Karen got the use of their dad's pickup and were there to lend a helping hand. They were packing and loading the vehicles with everything in the old house. By ten thirty, they were ready to drive up with the first load. All during the morning, Gary glanced over at Lynda's house. Every so often he would see the drapes slightly part, leading to the speculation that they were being watched. He was a little apprehensive about bringing Karen along that day. He really didn't want to have a problem with the ex-girl-friend meeting the new one. Also, he had given a lot of thought to what his sister had said about Karen. Was he just a fad to her? Some temporary public relation statement due to his rise in popularity, all brought about from the defense of his out-of-control big mouth? Actually, he had more in common with her brother than he had with her. He was starting to prepare himself that this relationship really wasn't going to last.

They pulled up to the new house just before noon. Jimmy drove much faster than the other cars, and they arrived earlier then every-one else. Gary rushed in and found the rooms that his mom had told him about. One was right next to the bathroom, and the other was on the far north of the house, off the kitchen, separate from the other bedrooms. Big decision. Privacy or convenience? He decided on privacy. He quickly started to unload his stuff and stockpile it in that room. Twenty minutes later, when his sisters arrived, there was some debate between Donna and Gary over his claim of the room, but he had the defense that if he didn't take it, it was going to be Mom's home office. Donna was pissed, but she had to concede to his logic. Again, Gary had to get in the last word by whispering to his sister that he was doing her a favor by taking this room.

"You won't be tempted with sneaking Steve back here and taking advantage of the privacy."

She motioned him back so that she could whisper back. "If I hear any moaning coming from this room and it's not your voice, I'm busting in with a video camera, got it?" She smiled at Karen as she left the room.

"What was that all about?" Karen remarked.

"Just my sister acting like my mother again. Let's go help unload the rest of the furniture. It would be good to sleep on my own bed tonight."

"Hmmm, you lying on your bed...that would be nice to see."

"Down, girl, you won't be able to see me lying on my bed if you were in there with me." He grinned.

"Even better." She walked over to Gary and put her arms around him.

They started to kiss mildly, with slow, small kisses. The kisses became slower and longer as the lips were finally locked in harmony as both lost themselves in the moment. All their kisses became blended together as one long passionate kiss as their tongues danced back and forth between the two teenagers' mouths. The moment was halted, however, as Carol passed by the room, looking for his brother. She looked in and turned and yelled back to the others.

"I found them, Mom!" Carol started to laugh. "Hey, Gary, you know they make toothbrushes for that."

The two were a little embarrassed, but it could have been worst. What if his mom or aunt walked in on them? Gary looked at Carol with a look of concern and fear. "Shh...not a word. Got it?"

"Why would I tell on you? I don't care whom you swap spit with," Carol retorted and left.

They both went out to fetch the rest of the furniture. Jimmy was a little pissed that he had to wait for them and was ready to throw the stuff off the trunk into the driveway. They got the remainder off and in the room and set up to Gary's liking. Jimmy came up with some excuse to get out of the trip down for the next load, and he and

Karen took off. Besides, he couldn't help looking at Donna throughout the morning, and he was getting wild looks back from Steve, who noticed the attention he was giving her.

"Glad to see him leave. I was getting tired of him staring at your ass all morning," Steve told Donna as they drove off.

"Why, Stephen, are you jealous of that little boy?" she said quizzically.

"Hell no. But he was staring at you. He was pissing me off."

"Well, I didn't notice him looking. I was too busy keeping my eye on your cute ass. Don't worry about him, baby. Let him look. He can only imagine what I got in these jeans, while you, on the other hand, can taste it." She picked up a box and held it out for him to grab. "But later…if we ever get all this shit unloaded."

They finally got all the vehicles unloaded and left to go back for their second load. Carol made some remark about how white Gary's teeth looked, which was not picked up as meaning anything to anyone except Gary, who was ready to throw his little sister out of the car for saying it.

The rest of the day was very tiring as the heat of the afternoon bore down on the family movers. They got everything loaded and all gathered on the front lawn, looking at the house. Regardless of the heat, they all crowded together to say goodbye to the house that their father built. Gary broke away from the group and ran to the backyard. He came back carrying a grapefruit from the tree out back.

"What's that for, dear?" his mom asked.

"I'm going to plant the seeds from it in our new backyard. That way, it would be like taking part of the old place with us."

"That's you all over, Gary…always thinking," Mom replied with a smile.

They all climbed into the vehicles and started the drive to their new home.

*****

It took the following week for everyone to get adjusted to their new environment. Gary liked being able to step out the back door in the morning and actually smell the salt air blowing in from the east. It was Saturday morning, and there was no practice today. That was a good thing, too, seeing that he'd had stayed up until two in the morning, chatting online. He had a lot of catching up to do. Most of the talk was about school starting and how the summer went by too fast and all. Most of his friends up north didn't start school until the following week, but for Gary, his first day was on Monday. This was the last weekend of the summer for him. He knew what he was going to do: he was going to the beach. His mom and sisters were going to do some serious shopping today for school clothes and essentials for the new house. But Gary had to find a way out of it and get to the beach with his surfboard. There was no way he was going to get it on a city bus, and it was too long a walk to carry it all the way there and back. He had already tried Jimmy, but he wasn't in luck there. He tried his aunt, but she committed herself and Frank to go shopping with the girls. Mike didn't like to surf or the beach, so he was no help. He was running out of options.

He then remembered that Coach Lewis usually spent some time at the school on Saturday mornings. He started to have a plan. He threw on some shorts and sneakers and jumped on his bike to pedal over to the school. He had told his mom that the gym was opened and he needed to work on some conditioning on his legs in the weight room. She bought it. When he got to the school, he noticed the coach's car in the parking lot and let the air out of his back tire so it looked like he got a flat. He went in and just so happened to run into Coach Lewis.

"Hi, Coach, what's up?"

"Not much today, Gary. What are you doing here on a Saturday?"

"Waiting for Mike to get here. We're heading to the beach today on bikes, but I couldn't give him directions to my new house, so we're supposed to meet here. Figured it would be easier."

"Yeah, it would, I guess. Well, I haven't seen him yet. What time was he supposed to meet you here?"

"Nine. He's late. Can I use your phone a sec?"

The coach nodded his approval and pointed to the phone. Gary quickly dialed Mike's number. After he got him on the phone, he went through a series of questions, all of which were answered by the fact that Mike, for some reason, couldn't make it due to some last-minute changes. He hung up the phone with a disappointed look on his face.

"He's not coming. Well, I better be going. I have some pedaling down to the beach to catch up with the rest of the family."

"Let me walk out with you. I'm heading home now, anyway."

They reached the tree where Gary locked his bike to. Imagine his surprise to find that he had gotten a flat. He couldn't call his family because they were already at the beach. What was he going to do?"

"Hey, let's go. We'll throw it in the trunk and drop it by your house on the way to the beach."

"Wow, thanks, Coach! You sure it's no problem?"

"No problem. It's just a short detour for me."

They loaded up the bike, and away they went back to Gary's house.

They talked about the first day of school on Monday. But Gary changed the conversation on how he was looking forward to being able to surf this last day of summer vacation. The coach probably got more than he wanted to know, but he enjoyed the boy's enthusiasm. He unloaded the bike when they arrived and went to the garage door to unlock it. He raised the door and started to yell.

"They didn't take my board! Damn it!"

He threw his bike down in his imaginary anger. He stopped and backed up, shook his head, raised his hands in the air, and then dropped them to his side. He looked back slightly to see if the coach was paying attention and saw him get out of the car and walk toward him.

"They left you hanging there, huh, buddy? Calm down, it's not something to get all worked up about."

"But this was my last day to get out to the beach and surf." He turned to "hide" his discouragement from his coach.

"Take it easy, Gary, we can handle this. Got any rope around here? We'll tie it to the roof."

Gary quickly grabbed a piece of rope from the shelf while Coach Lewis picked up the surfboard to carry it to the car. Gary closed and locked the garage and was elated on his good fortune. This was working so well he felt a little guilty that it was so easy.

They made their way to the beach with no difficulty at all. He unloaded the board and said goodbye and thanks to his coach. He picked everything up and went to "look" for the rest of the family. Of course, the mall was several miles away. He figured he had the rest of the day to come up with a plan to get them to pick him and his board up from here and take him home. Right now, he was there for the waves.

Coach Lewis looked back and watched his new student struggle his way to the water's edge. It was worth the trip to see this small boy carrying this slab of fiberglass which was bigger than he was across the sand. It was quite a comical sight. However, it was both heartwarming and saddening for him to watch a child taking such enjoyment from life.

Charles Lewis had always been devoted to the enrichment of youth. That was what made him such a good coach and teacher. He hid well the painful memories of the death of his wife and unborn child. It had been ten years since they were killed in a traffic accident. The child, his son, would have been ten years old today if not for that fateful event. He watched Gary balancing the board, knowing that even though he was struggling, he was still enjoying himself. The joys and experiences of youth that only a father could watch and be proud of. But he was proud of all his "children." Being the head coach at SCC had given him the opportunity to look over and help many students reach out and touch their dreams. His job helped him fill the void left by the tragedy. Unknown to Gary, he didn't need to work that hard to ask the coach for help. Coach Lewis always jumped at those requests.

Gary, after about an hour in the water, had to take a breather. He took a couple of nasty spills and even hit the bottom once when he wiped out in shallow water. Although he was quite nimble on his feet and had a good sense of balance, he still wasn't a good surfer. His size, or actually lack of it, prevented him for standing on his own up in high winds that usually accompanied bigger waves. He sat down on his towel and watched the water and numerous scantily clad girls lying out across the beach under the Florida sun. He saw some familiar faces walking down the beach. He waved, and Michelle and Patti waved back and started to walk toward him.

"Hey, Gary, where's Karen at?" Michelle asked as he stood to meet them.

"Hi, Michelle, ah… Patti, right? Karen went shopping. I thought you girls knew what the others were doing all the time."

"Not everything. Oh, that's right, you haven't met my kid sister. Gary, this is Patti. Patti, Gary."

Gary quickly laid out his other towel on the sand. "Hey, let's sit down," he said as the three of them plopped down on the sand.

"So Karen let you come to the beach all by yourself to stare at all these girls here?" Michelle said to start the conversation.

"Hey, she doesn't own me. Besides, I came here to surf, not girl-watch." He couldn't help himself looking in Patti's direction when he said that.

"Wow, you surf? Is this your board?" Patti remarked.

"Yep, she's all mine. Do you two know how to surf?"

"Not me. You're not going to get me on one of those things. Patti here is the adventurous one."

"Oh really, adventurous, huh? My type of woman," Gary said as he shifted into flirt mode.

"Well, I never tried it before, but I've always wanted to. What does a girl have to do to get lessons?"

"Just ask. I'm not much of a surfer, but I am a good teacher. Let's go. You ready?" He got up and offered a hand to Patti to help her to her feet.

"Right now? I don't know…"

"Oh, come on, don't wimp out now!" Michelle exclaimed. "Get off your ass and try it."

She took Gary's hand and pulled herself up from the ground. She was about the same height as Gary. Patti was a very young girl, fourteen years old, and was starting at SCC as a freshman this year. He couldn't help but look into her beautiful brown eyes and was caught off guard when he saw that they were looking right at his. Her smile was what got to Gary next. That, along with that reddish glow which emerged from her cheeks as her fixation was noticed. Gary, too, was slightly blushed when he realized he had not let go of her hand yet although she was already standing on her own two feet. He released her hand and grabbed the board to start her first lesson.

Michelle hung out on the shore and watched her sister try her hand at thrill-seeking. She was a little concerned there that there was a small bit of connecting happening between Gary and her sister. After all, Karen was her best friend, and this was supposed to be her new boyfriend. But then she remembered what Gary said was right. Karen didn't own him. They just went out a couple of times, and she was a year older than him. She watched her sister as she tried to stand up on the board and quickly fell off a split second after she straightened up. Gary swam over to her and helped her on the board, and both were laughing and having a good time with the experience. Michelle had to admit, they did look good together.

Around two o'clock, a young boy came running up to them. Gary saw the resemblance and knew that he had to be their brother. Their mother was there to pick them up. Gary picked up his board and told the girls he was going to leave also as soon as he figured how he was going to get home with his board and all. Of course, the girls volunteered their mom to take him home. Besides, he really didn't want to end this day with Patti yet. He thought the time he spent with Karen was good, but with Patti, it was even better. He was drawn to being with her. He sat next to her on the way home and kept up the conversation to get to know her better. Her mother did what she could also to find out more about Gary at the same time. He found that he had been going to the same church every Sunday that they went to, but they went to an earlier Mass. The implication that he was a churchgoer was an asset to her mother. An asset that he secretly thanked his aunt for being so insistent in making sure he went.

They arrived at Gary's house just after his family did. He introduced Patti and her family to his and proceeded to unload his surfboard, which of course Patti offered to help him with. When they got to the garage, she wrote down her phone number on a piece of paper while Gary secured his board. He glanced out and saw Donna looking at him with a smile on her face. She started to nod and mouths the words, "Go for it". He smiled back to acknowledge her approval of his new friend. She gave the paper to Gary and thanked him for the surfing lesson and said goodbye.

"Call me tonight. I'll be home," she said as she walked back to the car.

"Damn, can't leave you alone for a minute, Gar. You're becoming quite the stud," Donna said emphatically. Gary just smiled.

"I'm not a stud. I just met them at the beach."

"Okay, let's get inside. Gary has some clothes to try on. By the way, how did you get to the beach in the first place?" They all proceeded into the house carrying all the day's purchases.

"Oh, I got a ride. It's a long story, Mom. You don't want to hear it all."

"Yeah, okay, you will give me the abbreviated version while you try these pants on."

"Mom, why did you have to buy me new pants, anyway? I have plenty to wear."

"No, you don't. They have to be navy blue trousers to meet the school uniform requirements."

"Uniforms? I have to wear uniforms at this school?"

"Wow, Mom, he is a genius. He caught on real fast with that info," Carol said sarcastically.

He looked at his sisters, who were fighting to restrain their laughter. Carol was slowly losing the battle. He had never given it much thought about school uniforms. "What kind of shirt am I going to have to wear?"

His mom pulled out the clothes from the bags and laid them out on the couch. She took a shirt from one of the packages, and Donna took it from her hand.

"Well, the Catholic teenage boys of today will be dressed in these all-white dress shirts proudly displaying the school emblem on the pocket," she said, patronizing him like some model for *Alter Boy Weekly*. She held up the shirt to Gary's chest as to size it against his stature. He seized it from her as she continued with her presentation. Mom and Carol sat down on the couch opposite Gary to watch this impromptu fashion show. She went over and picked up other arti-cles of clothing. "Now, to accent this beautiful shirt, we complement its attractiveness with this solid navy blue tie. Notice how the tie matches the pants exquisitely?" She brought him a pair of pants and tie and displayed it against him like she did the shirt. "And to fin-ish off the ensemble, no Catholic boy's uniform would be complete without a pair of black dress shoes. Notice with that high-gloss finish that a young boy could see up a young girl's skirt from the reflection off these shoes."

Carol and Mom started to applaud her presentation. Carol was almost in tears from laughing.

Gary was getting pissed, though. He was going to look like a dweeb. All he needed now was a pair of dark-rimmed glasses and a pocket protector and he would be ready to be the nerd he always tried not to be.

"Hey, little bro, lighten up, we're just fooling with you. All the guys are going to be wearing them, so you won't look any different than anyone else. Besides, on you, these clothes could become quite the fashion statement."

Gary, as always, started to think about everything she just said. He picked up on one point distinctly. "What did you say about the girls wearing skirts?"

"Oh, you heard that, huh? Well, the girls wear these navy blue skirts and white blouse with the emblem. You'll be able to see as much of Patti's legs as you saw today. You should enjoy that."

Mom didn't. "Donna, stop now! Don't go putting things in his mind like that. Okay, show's over. Gary, go jump in the shower and get all that sand off, so you can try these on."

Gary complied with his mother's wishes and started toward his room. Carol was just starting to get control of herself and passed him on her way to the kitchen. She still had the giggles and was still quite amused that her brother had to wear school uniforms. He had to do something to ruin her mood. After all, that was his job as an older brother. If he couldn't enjoy it, why should she?

"What are you still laughing for?"

"I just think it's funny, that's all."

"Well, you won't for long. I found out from Karen that once one kid in the family gets into the school, the other kids don't have to wait as long to get accepted. You could be going to SCC in two years." He stepped back and scanned her body. "Yeah, I think you would look really cute in one of those blue skirts. Where is Mom? I have to go tell her."

Carol's face began to turn white. "Gary, *no*! Don't. Please?" She ran around her brother to intercept him. "Please don't tell Mom that, please."

She gave him the most pathetic, desperate look any eleven-year-old could give. Gary looked at his little sister and gave her a small smile. "Okay, I won't, but I better not hear any more comments about my uniform. Got it?"

"Got it." She went back around him, back into the kitchen, and stopped and turned back toward him. "You weren't really going to tell her, were you?"

"You'll never know. I'd only do it because you really would look cute in that skirt. But then again, you look cute in almost anything you wear, so you shouldn't get all worked up. But thanks, anyway. I like to watch you squirm." Now he felt better. He turned and walked into the bathroom.

After Gary tried on all his new wardrobe and dinner was over, he retired to his room for a night of online chatting. It was almost seven o'clock, and he was going to meet up with Mike online to go over the day's activities. As he sat down at his desk, he saw the note with Patti's phone number on it. He also thought that he should call Karen and tell her about his day with Patti and Michelle, before Michelle talked to her and she took it all the wrong way. He started to backpedal and rethink his plans for the evening. He went online and left a message to Mike that he was going to bed early tonight and he would have to call him tomorrow sometime. He then called Karen and found it was too late; she was already told about the surfing lessons. She didn't seem upset about it, though. He wasn't sure if that was a good thing or a bad thing, but he took it as a pass as far as a problem. He called Patti next and talked briefly about what classes she had this year and confirmed that she would be at the eight o'clock Mass. After he hung up the phone with her, he decided that he would just read to wear out his mind and get to sleep early tonight so he would be up in time to go to the early Mass. His mom and aunt would flip if they knew that he was looking forward to going to church on Sunday morning. He really didn't mind going. He felt closer to his father there. Believing in God and knowing that in his faith, his own father was in heaven, watching and waiting, drove him to strive to be a better person and try to always do the right thing, although it was his hormonal surges that made him more inclined to be there to see Patti again. Whatever the reason, the parts of Gary's life which had been the most stressed over this summer were coming together.

CHAPTER 10

Gary stopped and looked in the mirror and was really upset with what he was looking at. His buttoned collar was too tight, his tie dangling down to his waist, and the emblem staring at him from his top pocket were all too uncool. If his old friends saw him now, he would be the butt of all their jokes for the rest of the millennium. He dragged a comb across his hair to complete his new look and walked slowly from the bathroom. He was greeted with the usual compliments from his mom on how great he looked. Donna took her shots, while Carol just remarked that he looked good in his new uniform, with a serious, noncomedic demeanor. Gary sat down to have his breakfast and took it all in. He did grin inwardly on how naive his little sister was. She believed him so much that she could be a future candidate for this embarrassment. Donna volunteered to take Gary to school. With public schools starting the next week, she was available, and besides, she really wanted to see her brother walk into his new school. Gary, in the last year, had become quite overconfident and cocky, but now he was a little scared and apprehensive. It was a different look for him, and she picked up on it. She did enjoy a little watching him in this pensive mood, but deep down she was a little concerned also. She did what she could to get him to lighten up a bit during the drive to school, but Gary, as usual, was deep in thought.

"Gar, whatcha thinking about?" she said in a concerned tone of voice.

"Nothing!" he barked back at her for interrupting his train of thought. He was scared. A little more than he thought he would be. He was walking into a new environment that he wasn't used to. What more, he was also figuring that he would be dealing with more people of his intellectual standards. Before, he was the smartest kid around. Now he was going to be more of an equal. He kept trying to convince himself that he wasn't that vain to put himself as such high regards among his former classmates and school. But he always was; no matter how hard he tried to be just like everyone else, he always just stood out academically. Maybe this was what he really needed. The challenge was upon him once again. With fear as his ally and this stupid-looking tie as his shield, he was moving on to this new adventure. He was working at building up a positive attitude before arriving at his new battlefield of education when Donna spoke and stopped his momentum.

After the car stopped at a red light a block from the school, she tried again to confront her brother on his deep thought.

"Here," she said as she reached over and undid the top button of his shirt. "Now you can breathe a little better, so you can talk to me."

"What? What do you want to talk about?"

"I asked you what you are thinking about. I didn't think that was too difficult to answer, is it?"

"I was just thinking about school, that's all. Why do you want to know?"

"Just curious, that's all. You're always thinking about something, and right now you seem to be thinking about a lot of it." The light changed, and she started to drive through the intersection.

"It's just about school, that's all."

"That's all, that's all. It's just the first-day jitters. You'll be fine. By tomorrow this will be just the same old shit as you were used to back at South Kendall. So will you relax a little?"

"Yeah, but you will see what's it all about next week when you start."

"Yeah, but by then, you will be there to calm me down." She smiled a small grin as she approached the school ahead of her.

"Let me off here. I'll walk from here." He started to collect all his belongings.

"Oh, okay, now I get it. You don't want to be seen being dropped off by your big sister, huh?"

"No, it's not that. It's just that… I don't know. I guess I just want to walk into the school like I've always been there…not shuttled in like some lost new kid."

"Oh, okay, get the hell out and make your entrance, Mr. Moran," she said as she stopped abruptly as per his request. "Have fun today, and cheer up. You know that Dad is watching you, so don't be so uptight. You'll be fine."

He got out of the car with a small smile on his face. His sister knew him too well. With his notebook in one hand and his gym bag in the other, he walked through the gate to his new school. He already got a good feel of the place this summer, but that was when there wasn't anyone hardly there. Now the halls were packed with students, and this was much like he remembered it last year, when he was a freshman at Kendall for the first time. He remembered that he told himself that day would be the only time he had to deal with the experience. He was wrong about that one.

He pulled out his class schedule, read it quickly again, and then stashed it back in his pocket. He wasn't going to look like a lost student. He made his way to the sophomore wing of homerooms and started to proceed to his assigned room. He was making his way through some guys walking by him when one of the boys stopped him abruptly with a firm shove of his hand against Gary's shoulder.

"Hey, where do you think you're going? You lost or something?"

"No, that's my homeroom right there," he answered quickly with conviction.

"I don't think so. Little freshmen like you belong over there," the boy said as he pointed in the other direction. He was the biggest of the group of six boys that were now surrounding him. He decided that he wasn't going to tolerate his belligerence, but he had to come up with some alternative since he was grossly outnumbered, and he wasn't looking to get into trouble the first day of school.

"Oh, I'm sorry, but I do believe that freshmen's homerooms are over there," he said, pointing in another direction other than the boy had shown him. "You must be new here, or you would have known that. My room is right here." He moved past the boy and started toward the door. He felt a quick jolt on his upper back as he went flying forward, falling toward the ground. He was caught completely off guard by the attack but somehow managed to get his hands out to break his fall.

"Hey, we got us a little smart-ass here," the boy said as he approached Gary on the ground.

Gary rolled over and sprung to his feet before the boy could reach him. His football training had helped him there. He backed away from the boy as he neared but didn't run. He'd been in fights before, and he knew that running from this guy wasn't going to help him.

"Let us show you how we take care of smart-asses here."

Gary took a defensive position and stood his ground. "Us? What's the matter, you need help beating up someone smaller than you?" He knew he had to keep this one-on-one or he would be in big trouble, and he had used this tactic before to ensure it.

The boy reached at his arms, and despite his swinging them to avoid capture, he was grabbed, swung, and thrown into the arms of the other boys. The leader moved toward Gary and landed a punch to his midsection. He gasped for air, only to again lose it with the following repeated assault.

"We don't like smart-asses here, little boy. Now we'll really teach you a lesson—"

"Hey! Let him go!" someone yelled behind them.

Gary was released and fell to the ground as the boys took off. He heard the sound of running feet toward and away from him but couldn't get up to see who was coming or what was happening. He was dazed and confused. He couldn't breathe and was trying to catch his breath. He remembered briefly two hands grabbing him and rolling him down on his back, and then felt his waist rise as he was lifted by his belt to help him regain his air. He opened his eyes to see Jimmy standing over him.

"You okay?" he said as he looked down at him.

"Yeah, but get me off this ground, will ya?" he replied. He was helped to his feet and found himself surrounded by half the senior football players. That explained why the other boys ran. He couldn't believe this had happened, and on the first day too.

"What's going on here?" was the next thing he heard as the crowd started to suddenly disperse. He looked up, and there standing in front of him was a stern-faced woman in her forties, wearing a modest dress and carrying a clipboard full of papers.

Jimmy spoke quickly. "He's okay, Sister Jean, he just—"

"Fell!" Gary interjected. "I didn't want to be late, and I was running to get to my homeroom, and I must have slipped on something."

"Hmm, okay…right…let's get those scrapes looked at. Come with me," she said with a skeptical look. "The rest of you, go to class."

The remaining onlookers left immediately.

"I'll be okay, Sister. They are just little scrapes. I'll take care of them fast in the restroom there. My homeroom is right here."

"Okay, fine. You're new here, aren't you? What's your name?"

"Gary Moran, and yes, this is my first day here."

"Oh, yes, I think I have you in my algebra 2 classes this morning."

"Yes, Sister, that's my first period. Math is one of my best subjects."

"Good. Go clean yourself up and get to your homeroom. I'll see you in about fifteen minutes, then."

"See you then, Sister," he said as he started to walk away.

"Oh, and, Gary?"

He stopped and turned.

"I hope you are better at math than you are at telling the truth…" She gave him a stern smile and sent him on his way.

He rushed into the bathroom at the end of the hall and quickly cleaned himself up. He looked at his new white shirt, which was now dirty on one shoulder where he hit the ground. All he could think of was how mad his mom was going to be about it. He did what he could to wipe off the dirt from his shirt and pants, tucked in his shirt, readjusted his tie, and combed his hair. Well, he didn't look as geeky now as he did this morning, so maybe getting roughed up helped his outlook a little. He picked up his notebook and gym bag and left to go to class just as the first bell rang. He made it to his homeroom just as the teacher started to introduce himself. He found a seat quickly as he received a stern glare from the teacher showing his disdain for his tardiness.

"Good morning and welcome back to SCC," he said, breaking into a smile. "For those who don't know me, my name is Mr. Thompson. I teach English here at SCC, and for those who are truly lucky, some of you will probably have to deal with me again sometime today." His attempt at levity was welcomed with small laughter as everyone settled in for the start of another school year.

Mr. Thompson was a tall lanky Black man with a bald head and wide smile. It was apparent that he was at one time an athlete, perhaps in his younger days. He came across as a likable guy, firm but flexible. That was just the kind of teacher that Gary liked. He always had problems with the stern, power-driven people who usually had no sense of humor. Then there were the ones who tried to be overly open to the point their abundant exuberance took away from their credibility as a person there to give instruction rather than conformity.

He started to relax a little now. The day had just begun, and already he'd been through a lot. He could only hope it would get better.

Soon after attendance was taken, the bell rang, which was a signal for change of classes. As he made his way to his next class, he ran into Karen.

"Are you okay? Jimmy told me what happened." She tried brushing the dirt out of the arm of his shirt, with no noticeable improvement.

"I'm fine. This day is really sucking so far."

"It will get better. We better get to class. Meet me by the gym right after school before you go to practice, okay?"

"Sure, see you outside the gym later."

He met up with his cousin and Mike during lunch. He got the rundown on the bullies who beat him up that morning from Frank. The leader was a junior named Mark Katt. He was the typical underachiever who made up for his shortcoming by berating and bullying others. With his band of followers, they gained strength in the latter part of the previous year. The fact that his family had money and influence was perhaps the only thing that allowed him to return. This was going to be a thorn in Gary's side. He had always been able to avoid this kind of trouble, but now it had found him first. This was going to be on his mind while he continued his lunch.

But just then, he looked up and saw Patti looking at him from across the room. She was staring and, upon being discovered, quickly looked away. Gary smiled at the attention. This was a much-needed distraction to take his mind off his current dilemma. He spent the rest of the lunch period thinking of her. He watched as she stood up from the table and walked over to a nearby trash can. She glanced over and now caught him staring at her. Gary, however, did not look away. He waved and mouthed the word *hi*. She smiled and walked back to her table. He could not help but look down at her legs exposed beneath her short skirt. The shape of her breasts was translucent through her clean white blouse. He started to realize how much he had missed last year with the girls at his former school in jeans and oversized T-shirts. The uniforms helped very much in the enrichment of a young boy's imagination.

Just then, the bell rang, and they all got up to go to their next classes.

*****

A sigh of relief came to him at the sound of the last bell of the day. The remainder of his day had been well uneventful, relatively. He made his way through the rush of escaping students and got to the gym, where he was to meet Karen. She was there, waiting for him and talking with some other friends. As he approached, the other girls walked away, leaving her by herself by the time he reached her. He sensed a bit of uneasiness in her expression and realized he was about to get dumped. He knew the look. However, this time he was much more prepared and eager for the event. He went up to her and gave her a quick kiss and a smile.

"So how was your first day?" he asked to make for a light conversation before the talk got serious.

"Same as always. Not as exciting as yours was. How's your stomach feeling? And your shoulder?"

"They're fine. I've been thrown around before. I'm a survivor. So what did you want to talk to me about?"

"About us." She hesitated for a moment and then continued. "You know, I think you are sweet and cute and all…and I love the way you kiss, but…"

"But you don't think we are right for each other. Right?" Gary interjected with a solemn tone. He saw in her eyes that she was right, so before she could answer, he went on. "It's okay. I've been thinking the same thing. You know, I don't think I could have been able to get through today without having met you. A guy couldn't ask for any girl, especially one who is as beautiful as you, to be with and hold… to help initiate him into a new school like you did to me." He took her hand, and her frown turned into a small smile. He reached into his notebook and pulled out a piece of paper and handed it to her. "I wrote this poem for you."

She took the paper and started to read it silently.

A Friend Is Holding You

When times get rough and you can't move on,
Look ahead, a friend is holding you.
When you feel like falling and there's nothing to grab,
Look up, a friend is holding you.
When you can't go forward and feel yourself tumbling back,
Look behind you, a friend is holding you.
When you begin to cry as the world seems to close in,
Look beneath you, a friend is holding you.
When loneliness looks to take the day,
Look around you, a friend is holding you.
When a friend is there to keep you on your feet,
Look inside, you might find that it is you who are holding them.

When she looked up from the paper with tears in her eyes, Gary moved close and pulled her into his arms. He embraced her tight and spoke quietly into her ear. "The friendship you showed me this summer means more to me right now than anything. Thanks for making me fit in here. Without you with me this last month, I don't know how I would have survived this day." He released her from his grasp and kissed her on the cheek as they parted. "I have to get to practice. Today they tell us who made which team"

As her smile returned with her regained composure, she laughingly commented, "Duh, like I didn't know that!"

"Yeah, I forgot myself for a moment there. I already know that I'm not on varsity. Jimmy is a lot better than I am."

"Yeah, but then again, whether I'm at the varsity or JV game, I will still be cheering for the kicker in either game. Both teams will have the best. However JV will have the cutest one."

Gary blushed slightly at the remark.

She then added, "Boy, Patti is gonna be one lucky girl with you by her side."

"Huh, what's that mean?"

"You know what I mean. I know you got a thing for her, and I know she likes you, so don't be shy and go for it, stud. You two would make a cute couple."

"How did you—"

He didn't get a chance to finish before Karen jumped in. "Don't go defensive on me. I'm not mad at you for being normal. I'm not blind either, and her sister *is* my best friend. I think it's great. Just go slow, though, okay? She's never had a boyfriend before. You'd be great for her."

He thanked her for her insight and said his last goodbye again and ran to the locker room to change. The level of enthusiasm was extremely accelerated today, and Gary sensed it the moment he entered. There was a lot of talk on who was going on what team and who was going to be at what position. He put it out of his mind, though. He was confident that he was on the JV team and he would be the starting kicker. He hurriedly dressed and hustled on the field. Practice seemed less tedious than what everyone was used to. The truth was that the practice wasn't any different, but the added adrenaline flow due to everyone's anticipation just made it seem easier.

Coach Lewis gave his closing speech to the combined teams and told the boys that the lists were up in the locker room, and dismissed them. The boys seemed to run faster from the field than they did for the last two hours.

He made his way through the crowd among the cheers and sighs of his fellow teammates in front of him. He reached the varsity list first and scanned it for his name. Just as he figured, it was not there. He moved over to the JV list and looked down the list and was shocked not to find it there either. He looked again, and it was true; his name was not on the list. He started to think why he didn't make it. Did he do something wrong? How did he fail?

His train of thought was broken when he heard his name called and turned to see Coach Lewis standing by his office door. "Gary, go get changed and showered up and come see me in my office after."

He complied with his directive and went to change. He took his time. He was upset and wanted to try to calm down before he went to the coach's office and find out why he didn't make the team. Being one of the last to enter the showers, he was rewarded with the pounding of cold water on his naked flesh. This day was becoming a real nightmare. He was just wondering what else could go wrong today. His mind never stopped as he pondered on the impending possibilities.

He finally was dressed and was standing in front of the coach's office door. It was slightly open when he knocked, and a voice called him to come inside. Coach was sitting behind his desk, talking on the phone, when he motioned for him to sit down. He ended the conversation abruptly and hung up the phone.

"That was your mother I was just talking to. She's on her way here now to pick you up. First, I know you must be disappointed that you didn't see your name on the lists out there, but we have a situation here that we have to contend with."

"What situation?" he asked. His mind was going blank fast, not knowing where this was leading. He was prepared to accept that he was too small or not good enough, but not some "situation."

"Well, I was on the phone today with Mr. Browning, the principal of your old school. We must comply with certain regulations concerning transferring students, even when the students are coming from a public to a private school. The rule is that a transferring student is ineligible to compete in a sport program for one year unless a waiver is signed by the former school foregoing the sanction. Usually, this isn't a problem, but Mr. Browning is refusing to sign the waiver."

"Did he say why he won't?" He pondered his own question. He was destined to be a starter on the varsity this year there. His transferring left them with a hole on their special team squad. Was he being victimized for some personal vendetta for this shortfall? He didn't ask to be transferred like he was, and surely not for his football skills. He started to get agitated again as the coach confirmed his assessment of the situation just as he had surmised.

"Son, I even tried to reason with the fact that you didn't make the varsity team, that he was preventing you from playing a year in junior varsity, but he wouldn't budge. That's why I called your mother. We aren't through with this. I intend to fight him on this—that is, if you want me to. I know your passion for the game. You should be able to play if you want to."

"Of course I want to. I worked hard all summer long to make this team. I had figured that I would be on the JV team, but when my name wasn't there...well, I was a little..." He was fidgeting upon expressing himself bluntly to the coach. This was apparently not his fault, and he didn't want to go off on him. However, Coach Lewis was more aware of his feelings than he could know.

"Pissed?" Coach Lewis finished his sentence. "And you should be. It's okay to get a little mad, Gary. I'd expect that. You did work hard, and for a guy your size, you have more heart for this game than a lot of guys twice your size do. If I told you this before practice, you might have gone out there and hurt someone tackling them with your inner rage." His remark put a small smile on his face, although his mind was already trying to come up with an idea to get Mr. Browning to sign the waiver.

"So what do we do now? What's our first step?" he asked.

"Well, the first step is trying to do more reasoning with Mr. Browning. That's where your mother comes in. Let's let her appeal to him for your better interest and see if she can change his mind. If she can't, then we will have to go over his head. I don't like doing that. I wouldn't like it done to me, so I would like to avoid that avenue if we can. In the meanwhile, I would like you to keep working out with the JV team. The rule says you can't play, doesn't mean you can't still be part of the team. At least until we know that we can't get by this. What do you say?"

"Sure, I'd like that. I don't want to slow down any. If we can talk him into it, I'd be ready to start playing right away then."

"That's the plan. While we're waiting for your mom, how about helping me shut everything down here?"

Gary readily agreed. He was still feeling a little depressed over the whole ordeal, but the coach's talk did help. He knew his mom was going to tear into Mr. Browning as diplomatically as a woman enduring childbirth. A mother whose child is in pain does make a formidable foe, and he was in for the worst of it. He was already working on a plan to back up her offensive and overcome his setback.

By the time his mother arrived, he was calmer than he was earlier. He did not forget he had to get by his mother with the fight he had had that morning. The fact that his new shirt was still intact, although dirty, was going to be tolerated by his mother. That fact that he was in an altercation would be another matter, but he had to tell her about it. The fight was instrumental to his plan. He started to put in his mind that he was hurt from the fall. When he was out of the coach's sight, he worked on developing a "limp" as though his left ankle were hurting him. He limped around the corner just in time to see his mother talking to the coach. She saw him and waved. He waved back and started to limp toward them. His act was not noticed by either of them. They were too busy talking about him to pay attention to him. He went right by them, motioned that he was heading for the car, and proceeded toward the parking lot.

His mother talked highly of the coach on the way home. She commented on what a caring individual he was and how he seemed to really take a liking to her son. Gary was quiet on the way home, however, still working out his plan in his head. When they arrived home, his mother noticed his limp on the way into the house. He told her about the fight he was in that morning and how he must have twisted it. It had been bothering him all day long and couldn't kick during practice because it hurt when he tried to put his full weight on it. It was a lie. Due to all the problems that he encountered in his first day of school, his mother was less upset about the condition of his new clothes.

His sisters were attentive to his exploits as he described them. He did tell Donna that he and Karen broke up after school and had to admit she was right.

After dinner, he called Manny to see how the first day at his old school went. He told him about the fight and how he tore a tendon in his left ankle and he would probably be out for about five to six weeks. Another lie. He didn't mention anything about not being allowed to play due to the transfer restrictions. He knew Manny would spread the news around his former school about his unfortunate incident. That was the first step of his plan. He was going to make sure his mom didn't go talk to Mr. Browning for a couple of days, to ensure that the rumor was given enough time to circulate back to him. Another plan was in action, and Gary was on the offensive. He had more work to do in the next couple of days to pull it off.

CHAPTER 11

He had woken up early, got into the bathroom, and completed his morning grooming routine while the rest of the family was still in bed. He carefully wrapped his left ankle with a bandage and deliberately wrapped it with a slight incline on the heel to ensure that he would have to "limp" on it during the day. The set of crutches in his closet helped complete the charade. Imagine the surprise on everyone's face as Gary emerged from his room hobbling along carefully and sitting down gingerly at the table to have his breakfast.

"Gary, is your ankle hurting you that bad?" his mom said, being the first to comment on his condition.

"Just a little, Mom. It's okay. I just don't want to make it worse by walking on it."

"More like you want to get sympathy from the girls in school," Donna added. "He's gonna milk this for all it's worth, Mom."

"I don't need sympathy. I just want to take it easy on it, that's all." He was quick to defend his actions. "Besides, it's not like I'm gonna be playing, anyway, unless we can get Browning to sign that waiver, so I can afford to take it easy and let it heal."

"Hey, if you can't play right now, what does it matter if he signs it or not? Why push the issue with the old fart?"

"No way! Even if I can't play for the rest of the season, I still want that waiver signed. I worked hard to get on that team. If I can't play because of injury, so be it, but I am not gonna be told I can't play because someone won't sign a piece of paper." He had worked himself up to anger to push his position on the issue. He knew that if he could convince his family of his "injury," and regardless of the fact that he still wouldn't to be allowed to be active on the team, his plan was going to work with Mr. Browning.

"Well, Gary, I think maybe we should have the ankle checked out to see just how bad it really is. Aunt Connie has a family doctor up here that Frank goes to. I will see if I can get an appointment with him this afternoon to get it checked out. I will pick you up after school, and we will get it checked out," Mom said, with that being the final word on the subject.

Gary ate his breakfast and hobbled off to school. Donna dropped him off at the main gate this time. His need to appear helpless was to be apparent today in contrary to his previous day's attitude. He made his way to his homeroom as difficultly as he could. The looks were such that he was indeed going to get the sympathy that his sister foretold of earlier. He noticed the same group of boys that roughed him up standing in the same place as they were yesterday. He made his way around the group, giving the leader a quick glance of disgust for the "condition" he was in due to him. None of them gave Gary a second look as he went by. His plan had a secondary effect that he had not counted on. The guilt factor on his attackers weighed heavily enough to prevent another encounter with the bully or his gang. He kept his smile buried within as he grimaced in pain as he sat down at his desk.

He made it through the morning with little effort. He made light of his injury so as not to make anyone too interested and take notice of his true condition. The biggest test came at lunchtime, when he was approached by Patti. He told her his story as she sat there and listened with all too much concern with his well-being. This was definitely the sympathy his sister had commented on earlier this morning. He was not at ease to be sitting there and lying to her like that. He did like her, and if she discovered the truth later, it would ruin any chance he might have had. But he was committed to his plan, and it was necessary that no one know the truth. He did take advantage of the situation and asked her out Saturday afternoon to go see a movie. She, of course, accepted. He would have preferred to go to the beach, but in his "condition," he couldn't very well go surfing. He was contented enough that he was going to spend the day with her.

He made it through the day having convinced everyone, even Coach Lewis, that he was incapacitated. His mom had come to pick him up as she had told him she would. The doctor visit was extensive as to include X-rays to the whole ankle and foot, but the doctor could not find anything wrong with it. However, every time he pressed, prodded, or turned the ankle at the same point over the heel, Gary winced in pain. The only thing the doctor could come up with was a slight strain of a tendon in his ankle and prescribed an anti-inflammatory medication and the continuation of the restricted use Gary had already induced on himself. This was going just as planned. Now he had a diagnosis that he was not able to play. The story was set, and he had just to wait until Friday for the scheduled meeting with Mr. Browning to see if it was going to work.

Throughout the week, Gary continued his act. At the same time, he got acclimated with his new school and new teachers. The uniforms were something to get used to, but everyone was wearing them, so they were starting to grow on him. The curriculum was a little harder than he was used to, but then he had expected it so. It was not the difficulty of the material that made it harder but the accelerated rate of comprehension that it was going to be taught. His ability to learn was now at a level that his mind could accomplish. This was indeed what he needed academically. What he didn't need was his athletic time disrupted by some disgruntled school administrator who felt that his old school was being shafted by Gary's golden opportunity of an advanced education. He missed going to practice during the week. He had gotten to enjoy the practices, and he was gaining new friends and new acceptance every passing day. By Thursday night, he was ready for tomorrow's confrontation. He settled into his room for the night and decided to take his mind off the week's events with a little online chatting. He cruised the chat rooms for a while and got into some good conversations on the others' "start of school" happenings. Needless to say, his story was far more intense than most. In a short while, he noticed Kim's screen name on his buddy list and quickly instant-messaged her.

> **Pkicker:** *Hey you!! Whasup?*
> **Chickee89:** *Hey, stranger. Nada. How ya been? How's school?*

Pkicker: School's great. I have to wear a stupid uniform but I'm dealing with it.

Chickee89: Let me guess, white shirt and tie?

Pkicker: Yeah, how did you know?

Chickee89: I just know how Catholic boys dress. There's a school up here just like it. I want a pic of you in your uniform.

Pkicker: Not gonna happen.

Chickee89: Oh, come on. I bet you still look cute. How about a pic of you and Mike together?

Pkicker: Now you are really dreaming. Like Mike's gonna go for that.

Chickee89: Sure, why not. Is he ashamed of what he looks like?

Pkicker: No, he's just a little shy online, that's all. He's much different in person. He just doesn't get too personal online and a picture to him is too personal.

Chickee89: Ok, so he's not so cute. I still want a pic of him.

Pkicker: You are way off. He's better looking than me.

Chickee89: ok, prove it. You send me a pic of him.

Pkicker: ok, ok, I will see what I can do. Don't start bitching at me now. I know you women like to bitch until you get what you want.

Chickee89: I don't bitch. I nag. If you piss me off and get me yelling, then I bitch. So, don't push it, bud!

Pkicker: Yeah, yeah, now I'm really worried. LOL. No promises but I will try to get a picture scanned and send it to you.

Chickee89: Good. So, how's your leg? Mike told me you got hurt.

Pkicker: It's just a sprain. Doesn't matter though, I can't play right now anyway.

Chickee89: Why not?

Pkicker: *The principal at my old school won't sign the waiver letting me play. Transferring students have to sit out a year before playing sports at the new school.*

Chickee89: *Well, that sucks! So, does that mean I will be catching you online earlier after school for now on?*

Pkicker: *Nope, I'm not done fighting yet. My mom and I have a meeting with him tomorrow afternoon to talk him into signing the waiver.*

Chickee89: *You think you can get him to change his mind?*

Pkicker: *I think so.*

Chickee89: *Oh, no, you're dangerous when you start thinking. The asshole won't know what hit him.*

Pkicker: *Damn, girl, you haven't even met me, and you know me too well.*

Chickee89: *Yeah, I will meet you in December. If your girlfriend lets you. LOL*

Pkicker: *I don't have a girlfriend right now. So, you're safe. LOL.*

Chickee89: *What happened to Karen?*

Chickee89: *And what does that mean, I'm safe? Safe from what?*

Pkicker: *First of all, Karen and I broke up, it was mutual so no big deal. What I meant that I don't have a girlfriend, so it would be safe for ME to meet you.*

Chickee89: *Oh, ok, I don't care how many girl-friends you have when I get there. I just want to meet you. I'm not taking you back up north with me.*

Pkicker: *Oh, use me and abuse me, just don't keep me. I see how you are.*

Chickee89: *Exactly, now you got it.*

Pkicker: You mean you won't take my virginity back up there with you? LOL
Chickee89: Hell no!! If the girls down there don't want it, why would I? LOL
Pkicker: Now that was cruel.
Chickee89: No, cruelty is what happens if I don't get a picture of you and Mike in your uniforms.
Pkicker: I said I will try so stop bitching.
Chickee89: Ok, I have to go anyway. Talk to you again this weekend. Bye.

Gary signed off and went over his game plan for tomorrow's confrontation. He was careful not to tell Kim too much about the truth of the injury. He needed to keep his plan secret. Regardless of the outcome of his scheming, he never told anyone of the fact that he had planned anything at all. He had always been successful due to the secrecy that he always maintained. No one could counter a plan if they didn't know one existed. Even though Kim was several hundred miles away, he could not take the chance of her telling Mike. She also posed a new challenge to him. How could he get a picture of Mike and himself, in uniform, to send to her? That was something he had to work out later. That, plus working up the nerve to meet her if she did come down to Florida like she said she would. He was not sure if he could be the same person in person as he was online.

He got to school a little earlier than usual. He limped his way to Coach Lewis's office to gain some moral support for the conference with Mr. Browning that afternoon. He was relieved to have heard that the coach was still pushing to have him being allowed to play this year even if it was on the JV squad. The coach's call on the previous day to his former principal might not have gotten the job done, but it was noted that there was some concern for Gary's injury. Somehow, he had heard that Gary had hurt his ankle and was on crutches. He pondered with the coach just how he found out about that. Inwardly, he was beaming with joy on how his plan was coming together.

He went on to his classes, hobbling around the morning the best he could. He followed his assignments as well as he could, although one of his teachers did take notice that his mind was preoccupied. And it was. He was working up in his mind a certain attitude to unleash on the unsuspecting Mr. Browning. He was going into the meeting that afternoon part pissed off, part disappointed, and with a large amount of pain. He had the morning and the three-hour drive to Miami to work it up to the desired tempo.

It was eleven thirty when his mom arrived to pick him up. She was all too ready to go to this meeting without her son, but he wouldn't hear of it. He wanted to go and defend himself. She had been handed volleys of reasoning from him all week long. *"This is my problem. I should be able to handle it." "There's no reason for him not to sign that waiver, and if there is, I want to hear it directly from him." "If he is going to say no, I want to hear him say it to my face."* He was adamant about going, and she wasn't going to deter him. She did have a certain confidence in her son. He had been one with conviction when he was set off, and this was one of those times.

They arrived at the school at two forty-five, a little early for their three o'clock appointment. Gary ran into a few friends and went over his story again about his "injury." Of course, this time he left out the part of getting hurt while being beaten up by a bunch of bullies but changed the cause to his rough play as a defensive back during practice.

They made their way to Mr. Browning's office, where they were shuffled right in and sat down. Gary sat down slowly, of course, maintaining his act for his new audience. After all the congenialities were exchanged, Mr. Browning was fast to start into the matter at hand.

"Well, I know why you came to talk to me today, Gary, but I have to stand by the rules to keep things fair with transferring students."

"Excuse me, sir, but how is not allowing me to play JV football being fair?" Gary jumped in, maintaining a firm but cordial tone of voice.

"It's fair because it makes sure that schools don't gain an unfair advantage by gathering up and transferring students for the benefit of their athletic programs."

"My son didn't transfer there to play football. We applied there five years ago to give him a more challenging education, like it was recommended that we do from you own school district counselors," Mrs. Moran said with a stern force behind her words.

"Here, Mr. Browning." Gary pulled out a piece of paper and handed it to him. "That is the very letter where the school board suggested that I be transferred into a special school with a gifted student program, and it's dated February of 2004. Almost five years ago. By transferring to SCC, I'm not doing anything different than what was recommended by your school board."

"This has nothing to do with this rule. It has to do with athletic eligibilities for transferring students. Even if you were transferring to another public school, you would still have to be ineligible for one year at your new school. That's the rule, and you can't get around it."

"Excuse me, sir, but you can. Why would they even give you an option of signing a waiver which would allow me to play? I don't understand why you just won't sign it. Why are you afraid of letting me play football? I'm not going to be some future NFL professional." He was going stronger now; his voice was growing tense.

"That's just it, Gary. You're not, and with your leg hurt like that, why do you feel so emotional that you have to be an exception to the rule?"

"Sir, this leg is exactly why I need to be allowed to play. I used to get laughed at and picked on just because I was so smart. I don't try to be, but I just am. I'm the nerd, the teacher's pet, the short skinny runt that gets beaten up for the hell of it. Did you hear? That's how I got hurt. Five guys on the first day of school used me as a punching bag, and they don't even want to play football. I do. It's the one thing that makes me get some respect. It makes me like everyone else instead of something different. Even if I can't play because of this"— he pointed to his ankle—"I still want to able to know that regardless of injury, I can still be, and should be, able to be part of the team that I worked hard all summer to make. I didn't even make varsity, only

JV, but I still made it. I may not be able to walk on this right now, let alone kick with it, but that should be my call to make, not yours. Can't you just sign the waiver and let me have that option?"

Mr. Browning looked sternly at Gary for a moment, taking in his speech, its content and delivery. Mrs. Moran just sat there looking proudly at her son for having said it all so profoundly.

Mr. Browning sighed, looked down at his desk, and then again back at Gary, breaking into a small smile at the sight. There was a small intelligent young man sitting there with more passion for life than men bigger and older than him. It was a hard act to fight. "Gary, I just hope that South Central Catholic knows just how lucky they are to have you as a student. I'll get the waiver signed and send it up to your coach."

"Thank you, Mr. Browning, but that won't be necessary." Gary pulled another piece of paper out of his pocket and handed it to him. "I brought a waiver form with me."

"Hmm, you were that confident that you'd get me to change my mind?"

"No, sir, but I figured that if you did, it wouldn't hurt to be prepared."

Mr. Browning chuckled at the boy, signed his name on the form, and called in his secretary to have it notarized. Gary was overjoyed that his plan worked, but still maintained his act, cautiously rising from his seat using his crutches for support. After a short conversation on how Gary liked his new school and what his classes were like and such, they said their goodbyes and made their way to the parking lot.

He ran into Manny and a couple of other former teammates, whom he got to talk briefly with while Mom brought up the car. He maintained his story right to the very end while he crawled into the car in front of them.

They had gotten on the highway when his mom decided to confront her son on his performance.

"You handled yourself pretty good back there, young man. How bad is that ankle of yours, anyway?"

"Oh, it hurts a little, but I will be okay."

"Yeah, I'm thinking that it will probably get better really soon now. Am I right?"

"Yeah, probably." He paused a second to ponder her inquiry. "When did you know?"

"Oh, I caught on when you sat down in the office back there. You were moving better than that for the last two days. You became a downright cripple when you tried to sit down in front of Mr. Browning. I can't believe you went through all this just to play football."

"Come on, Mom, I wasn't really lying back there. Playing football does gain me some respect with guys bigger than me. If it weren't for football, the senior players might not have stepped in and stopped those guys from wailing on me. Are you mad at me?"

"No, I'm not mad. That old windbag needed to be taught a lesson there. It did feel good to be on the other side of one of your con jobs for a change." She gave him a big smile and a gentle rap on the back of his head. "I'm getting pretty good at figuring you out, so you better watch it."

They made it through rush hour traffic and arrived home in time for the dinner that Donna was home preparing. Gary was too excited to really eat; he ate as quickly as he could, but enough of it as to not upset his sister for her efforts. He then went to his room and booted up the computer.

He had already tried to call Mike, but the phone was busy. He assumed Mike was probably online, so he figured to talk to him there. After he signed on, his assumptions were confirmed. Mike was there, and so were Kim and Lisa. They were all in a private chat room, and he was immediately invited to join them. The conversation was short and informative. He got to tell them about his success in solving his problem. Mike jumped in and asked how long he was going to be out before he was going to be able to play, especially now that he could. He told them he should be able to play in about a week, although he refrained from telling them that he was probably going to have a sudden recovery in lesser time. The rest of the conversation led on to a more congenial tone until Donna knocked on the door to tell him he had a phone call. He said his goodbyes and signed off. It wasn't until he got to the phone that his sister told him it was Patti.

"Hey, Patti, what's going on?"

"Nothing. Just wanted to see how you were doing. You know, with your leg and all."

"The leg is fine. I can even walk on it a little better now. You're not worried about me making our date tomorrow, are you?"

"No, I'm sure you wouldn't stand me up. However, you did keep me waiting on the phone a bit until you got here. What took you so long?"

"I was chatting online, and I had to sign off and all. Did I keep you waiting that long? I'm sorry, I signed off as fast as I could. Donna didn't tell me it was you until I got to the phone, or I would have just pulled the plug to get here to talk to you."

"What a load of…" She paused briefly and laughingly added, "Hmm, you are quite the flirter, Gary Moran, aren't you?"

"Hey, a guy is only a good flirter if there is someone special enough to flirt with."

"Oh, am I that special?"

"Of course you are. I'm looking forward to spending the afternoon with you tomorrow."

"Well, that's why I called you. My mom wants to know if you can come over to dinner after the movie, if you want to, that is."

"Sure, why wouldn't I? This means I get to meet your dad then, right?"

"Exactly. Hey, you are as smart as I heard you were."

"Thanks, I think. Your dad's not a really big guy, is he? Meeting girls fathers is not big on my lists to do."

"He's not anything like Karen's dad. He's a pussycat, so don't worry about it. Why do you say that, anyway? I heard you handled yourself really good at Karen's house the first time there."

"Well, that's because it was the first time I ever had to meet a date's father. It was all that I imagined. Mr. Taylor was quite an initiation to dating."

"You mean you never had to meet a girl's dad before? I heard you had a girlfriend in Miami."

"Yeah, but with Lynda—that was her name…well, it still is her name, but…" Gary was stuttering a bit talking about his former girlfriend like this. "Well, anyway, she lived across the street from me all my life. I met her dad before I could walk, so he doesn't count."

"How long did you go out with her?" she asked, and Gary dreaded having the conversation shift toward Lynda like this.

"About a year. But what about you? How long did you go with your last boyfriend?" Gary reversed the tables on her, already knowing that she had never had one, so that she would move off the subject.

"Never had one before. Never met anyone worthy enough."

"So does that make me worthy, then? You are going out with me," he said confidently.

"Worthy enough to go out with. A boyfriend? We will have to see about that. I have to check with my dad first?" She laughed softly on the other end of the phone. Gary was impressed with her quick, witty response.

"So you must be Daddy's little girl, then, huh?"

"Of course I am. I'm his youngest daughter, so you better watch it."

"If it's you I get to watch, it will be my pleasure."

"There goes that flirting again. Are you like that when you are chatting online?"

"No, mostly I just talk to friends from my old school and some from SCC. I've talked to a couple of people from around the country that I get along with and like to talk to. Do you have internet at home?"

"My dad has internet service that he uses for work. I don't know which one. I'm not really into it. I like picking up the phone and talking instead of sitting in front of a monitor and typing at a keyboard."

"But nothing beats talking face-to-face, especially if the face I'm talking to looks like yours."

"Oh, really now, and you know that much about my face to make that determination?"

"Oh, of course I do."

"Oh, okay, what color are my eyes, then?"

"Dark brown."

"Hmm, very good. Do you always notice things like that with the girls you know?"

"No, just the special ones."

"Now you are laying it on real thick, Moran. For someone who's only had…how many? Two girlfriends his entire life? You sure know how to sweet-talk a girl. You must get a lot of practice flirting with your online girlfriends."

"What? What online girlfriends? I don't—"

"Yes, you do. You don't have to slide around me. It's okay. I don't own you, so you don't have to go all defensive now. Besides, if what you learned online, you use on me to flatter me so, I'm cool with it."

There was some noise in the background, and Gary was told to hold on a bit while Patti went to see who wanted her. She came back within the minute to tell him that she had to get off the phone now and she would see him tomorrow.

After hanging up the phone, he went to his room to ready himself for bed. He started to ponder about Patti and what she had told him. Did he flirt that much? He did flirt online, but that was with girls he would probably never meet. He figured if she was right and it was a personality trait that he was forming, he had better make an effort to try to control it more. But in Patti's case, it was different, because he wasn't talking to her online and had met her face-to-face. He felt very strongly about what he had said to her, and it wasn't empty flattery but truthful admiration. Ever since he met her, she had been in his thoughts most of the time. With Lynda, he never had to think about her, because she was always there, and over time, he just became comfortable with her. Patti was a different story. He hadn't spent that much time with her except for that time at the beach, yet he had strong feelings for her. This was a little confusing for him, because it had no reasoning to back up these feelings. And the more he thought about it, the more it baffled him. In his mottled thoughts, he wondered if love was the reason behind his confusion. Could he be falling in love with Patti?

Tomorrow was going to be an interesting day.

CHAPTER 12

There was one thing Jerry hated more than the Florida heat; it was the hurricane season and the rains they brought. It had rained for the last three days, which was normal for South Florida in September. The last two months had been very hard on him and his team. Everyone except Lauren. Her job was sitting at a desk with several monitors and three keyboards as she talked online to unsuspecting targets. It was a lot of work, though. She sometimes had to chat as three different persons at the same time to give the illusion that they were all separate identities. She followed a timetable of online activities that Jerry had listed for her. Sometimes she spent hours talking to herself just to legitimize the identities. She had to watch the clock as to time of day in Vermont or other locations as compared to that of her targets. She had over forty online personas located around the country, and not all of them were female. Multiple conversations with several different genders tend to make it a safer comfort zone for her intended targets.

Jerry was standing behind her, watching her do her thing, and had always been amazed at how she made it all look so easy. She saw a quick reflection in one of the monitors and let out a small scream as she turned around, startled.

"Damn it, Jerry! Make some noise or something. I hate it when you sneak up on me and hover like that!"

"Sorry, darling. You were so engrossed in your flirting there I didn't want to interrupt you. Did that guy just tell you he wanted to take you hiking so he could fuck your brains out on the side of the mountain?"

"Yeah. Don't mind him. That's only Brian from Mt. Juliet, Tennessee. I don't think he's really sixteen, but I like to jerk his chain a bit."

"Well, drop him. If he is a perv and he's talking to others, he's liable to get caught, and then they will be looking for you as a witness. Give the IP address you are talking with him on to Miguel, so he can shut it down and block the connection. Stop wasting your time on shit like him. How's the Miami Beach target going?"

"Eddie told me we have a go with the warehouse in Opa-locka next week. The best time I can get with a possible meet time is September 29. I am supposed to be coming down to Miami Beach for my grandparents' sixtieth anniversary, and I told him that I will be staying at the Fountain Blue. He will ride his bike to meet me on the beach there."

"Eddie, how does that work for you?"

"That works out. There's a Jet Ski rental on the beach there. I purchased a small fifteen-foot boat with the bogus American Express card and have it parked over at Haulover Pier. On that day, you rent two Jet Skis and have Lauren take one of them to bring you out to the boat. I will be as close to the shore as I can and drop a line in to look like we're fishing. Lauren goes back in and waits for our target. The kid likes to Jet Ski, so, Lauren, just make sure he knows to look for the one on shore and yell at him to climb on and come and get you. As soon as he starts to follow, she makes a beeline out toward us. When she gets close enough, she will wipe out and go into the water. We will go to her rescue at the same time the target gets there. I will position the boat between them and the shore to block the view. We sedate the kid and bring him aboard. You and Lauren jump on the Jet Skis and return to shore. You both grab the van and meet me at the pier."

Then he continued, "Miguel, you're next. Do you have the accounts set up for the transfer?"

"All set, boss. I will have the account numbers ready for you. I have a round-trip plane ticket to Rio de Janeiro for the pickup. I secured a line that will bounce around the world a couple of times to deliver the ransom demands."

"Brazil, huh? I like it. Let's make that the same on the last one also. I hear that the beaches of Brazil are fantastic in December. Except that time, we will all be down there together."

Lauren let out a short scream of excitement. "About time! You have been promising to take me to Rio."

"Oh, you still want to go, or do you want to go meet Brian in the Tennessee Mountains for some outdoor sex attack?"

"Funny. No, you're the only perv I want to be with, and they have mountains in Brazil."

CHAPTER 13

Gary leaped out of bed, forgetting completely about his "injury." He threw some clothes on and had started to go out of his room when he remembered he was supposed to be hurt. He didn't bother wrapping the ankle and opted to just grab one of the crutches and hobbled out to the room. Everyone was already up and sitting at the table, eating breakfast. They watched as he made his way to the table and gingerly sat down. His sisters watched his actions in silence, and as soon as he sat down, they looked at each other and started to laugh hysterically.

"Put it away, Gary. Mom already told us about the act you've been pulling on everyone," Donna said as she was composing herself. "You should quit football and join the drama club."

Gary looked at his mother and felt betrayed. He looked at Carol with a stern look. "Don't you say anything about this to anyone." He moved closer to her and whispered, "Or else."

"Or else what? Are you gonna tell Mom that she can put me at that school because you got accepted and make me wear a uniform too? I checked it out and talked to Mom. It's not gonna happen."

"Wow, why did I get up this morning? I'm going to go back to bed."

"No, you are not, young man. Your ankle is fine. You can limp while pushing that lawn mower this morning."

"Aw, Mom. I thought you weren't mad at me."

"I'm not. The lawn still needs to get cut, and all the scheming you did this week didn't stop it from growing, so you better eat fast and get to it. Don't you have a date for the movies this afternoon with Patti?"

"Oh, yeah, Mom, I forgot to tell you. Patti called me last night, and her mom invited me over for dinner after the movie. I already told her yes. We didn't have plans for tonight, did we?"

"Nothing you can't get out of. Connie and Frank are coming over tonight. I'm making chicken Parmesan and a homemade cheesecake. We were going to celebrate your immaculate recovery. Too bad you are going to miss all that." She chuckled.

Gary was a little disappointed. His mom knew that chicken Parmesan was his favorite, and homemade cheesecake was hard to pass up. "I will have to pass on it tonight, Mom. Can you try to save me a piece of the cheesecake?"

"Oh my god! Gary passing up chicken Parm to go out with a girl! Someone's in L-O-V-E!" Donna said in a devilish tone.

Gary blushed and started to eat his breakfast. It was already eight thirty, and he had a lot of yard work to get done so he could get to the movie theater by two o'clock. He reiterated his desire for his sisters to keep quiet on the faking of his injury. They both said they would. Donna, he believed; Carol, though, was a loose cannon. He would have to work on her more through the weekend.

While he was doing his usual thinking of the past day's activities, he had realized that he would have to go back to the doctor to get a release form that his ankle was okay to play football again. He would have to pick the right time this weekend to inform his mother about that. She would not be happy about it.

He finished his breakfast and went to change into some old jeans and a T-shirt to get the yard work started. As hot as the morning was turning out to be, Gary moved with a determined pace to get all the work done. He found himself thinking more about Patti while he worked, which seemed to make the work go faster. After he finished the mowing in the backyard, he pushed the lawn mower around front to the garage to exchange it for the edger. To his surprise, Carol was out front, raking out the flower beds and around the bushes, putting all the debris in nice little piles. She stopped and gave a quick wave and kept working. Gary appreciated the help but was confused why he was getting it from his little sister.

"You must really be bored to be out here helping me like this in this heat."

"No, I just wasn't doing anything, so I thought I'd give you a hand."

"Okay, so you were bored, then." He chuckled. "Come on, tell me the truth. Why are you helping me?"

"Gar, you probably think I won't keep your secret, and I just want to tell you, this time I will. I know in the past I talk too much and gave things away on your schemes, but I know how important it was for you to beat Mr. Browning, and I think it was pretty cool how you did it."

"Well, thanks for the help, then. Don't go too fast now around the bushes up front. I still have to weed-eat around them, and I'm just going to get more cuttings around them, and we'd have to rake them again."

"That's good to know. Someday I will have to do this all by myself when you go to college."

"No, you won't. You will be just like Donna and find a guy like Steve to fall in love with you and do all this work for you. I thought Donna taught you all these things."

"Yeah, but I still have to learn how to do it so I can tell my guy how to do it."

"I don't think you were born. I think Mom and Dad just cloned you from Donna's DNA."

They both went back to work. He guessed his little sister was growing up, but that now meant he would have to watch her more than before. He was protective of his sisters regardless of their strong, independent demeanor. His dad would expect him to do it. He knew someday he would be the one to walk both down the aisle when they got married. He was the man in the family, and although he didn't ask for it, he took the job seriously.

He took a minute to look up and say, "I got this one too, Dad."

They finished up the lawn work around noon, and Gary jumped in the shower to wash the dirt and sweat off his body. He made a couple of sandwiches while Carol was taking her shower. It only seemed right to make lunch for her for helping him all morning. As he was sitting there, eating, he realized that the house was very quiet. It was then he remembered both Donna and his mother had left earlier and hadn't returned home yet. Who was going to take him to the movies? He ran for the phone and quickly called his mom. She had to go down to the office in Miami and wouldn't be back till late. By the time he got ahold of his sister, it was close to one o'clock, and he was starting to panic. She was busy making friends at some hole-in-the-wall nail salon and lost track of time. She was on her way. Great! His first date with Patti and now he might be late. He went in his room to get ready, and his computer monitor was blinking. He didn't have time to see who was looking for him online. He logged off and shut down the computer and started to get dressed for his date.

His sister arrived just as he was ready, and he rushed out of the house without letting her out of the car. He jumped in the car, slid the seat belt on, and yelled at his sister to go. Donna just sat there smiling.

"What are you waiting for? I do not want to be late."

"Hmm, really now." She hit the horn and waited. "You got everything you need? Are you missing anything?" Just then, the front door opened, and Carol walked out carrying his crutches with her. She locked the door and ran to the car with crutches in hand. Gary was embarrassed. He forgot completely about his ankle injury and that Carol was not going to stay at home alone. She climbed into the back seat and put on her seat belt.

"I'm good. Let's go." She laid the crutches across her lap and the back seat. "I got your back, bro."

Donna started to smile, holding back the laughter. It was not common for Gary to be so absent-minded. He was more flustered than on his first date with Karen. She asked him what movie they were going to see, but he didn't know. They didn't even talk about what movie they were going to see. He figured they would decide when they both got there. She informed him that Carol and she were also going to see a movie, so she wanted him to decide quickly and let them know so they could pick a different one.

They arrived at the theater promptly at two o'clock, parked the car, and Gary quickly adopted his "limp" with the help of his crutches. Patti arrived a few minutes later with her sister and younger brother in tow.

"So you brought chaperones with you also," Patti said with a smile.

"No, they will be going to a different movie than us. What about your entourage?"

"Don't worry, Gary. I'm here to take Brad to see the *Transformer* movie. If you don't go sci-fi, you won't see us." Michelle was quick to rest his mind at ease.

"That sounds good to me also, Gary. You two can have your pick of the other fifteen theaters," Donna added as she walked by him and went to the ticket counter to buy her tickets.

Gary let out a sigh of relief and let Patti pick the movie from the remaining list. He paid for the tickets and escorted his date inside. He bought popcorn and sodas and went into a dimly lit theater, where the previews had already started playing. They made their way up the steps to the back of the theater and moved across to the center seats of the row. They got comfortable and began to watch the movie. Halfway through, when the popcorn was gone, Gary decided to make a move. He remembered the warnings to go slow, and he was going to do just that. Very slow. He reached out his hand and slid it on top of hers, resting on the armrest between them. He rolled his hand under hers and cupped her hand into his. He was rewarded by feeling her increase her grasp on his hand, accepting his touch. Soon after, she rested her head on his shoulder. It was not a very comfortable position. He released her hand, grabbed the armrest, and raised it back between the seats. Raising his arm around her head, he placed it on her other shoulder and pulled her back into resting against him again. Taking his other hand, he reached over and again took her hand into his. He looked down and saw her smiling at him.

She whispered, "You didn't learn that move from the internet."

They both went back to watching the movie.

As they left the theater, they met the others out front. Donna and Michelle already coordinated the travel arrangements. Donna would follow them back to Patti's house so she would know where to pick Gary up later that evening. Donna had to remind him of the meal that he was missing back home. To his surprise, Brad perked up and said, "Hey, we're having chicken Parmesan also tonight." Gary could do nothing but smile at his sister. He hobbled over to the car and handed the crutches to Carol. "I'm going to go the rest of the evening without these." He limped back to Michelle's car and slid into the back seat next to Patti.

Dinner at the Fuscos' was quite an event. He got to meet Mr. Fusco, who was nothing like Mr. Taylor. A man of smaller stature but with a very big heart and a family to boot. They were a very atypical Italian Catholic family. Patti was the youngest daughter, but along with Michelle, she had an older brother and sister (twins), who were away at college, and two younger brothers, Brad (ten) and Anthony (seven). Mrs. Fusco was, as he expected, a very good cook. They had a big salad, homemade bread, chicken Parmesan, meatballs, rigatoni pasta, and homemade apple pie for dessert. He was hungry and ate what he could. Just like his grandmother or his aunt, Mrs. Fusco liked to push the food on you. He found out that this big dinner was only a one-night-a-week deal, usually on Sunday, but they pushed it up a day for Gary's visit. The food was very good.

After about an hour, Patti suggested that they take a walk to help digest everything they ate. He readily agreed because she was right; if he didn't get up and walk, he probably would fall asleep after a meal like that. Mr. Fusco himself already looked like he was ready to doze off any minute.

As soon as they got to the sidewalk, Gary reached out and took hold of her hand. She had never held hands before with a boy, but she liked holding Gary's hand. They walked down the sidewalk and talked about the movie, school, and the weather. As they turned the corner, Patti stopped and looked down at Gary's ankle.

"What happened to your limp? Doesn't it hurt?"

"Yes, a little. I stopped thinking about it when I'm with you."

"There goes that flirting again."

"I'm not flirting with you. I think you are smart and beautiful, and I wanted to ask you out the first day I saw you in the parking lot. I really like you, and I want to spend more time with you."

Gary reached out and took her other hand and pulled her close to him. He leaned over and pressed his lips on hers. She did not pull back. He looked at her eyes, and they were closed, so he again pushed forward and kissed her again. This time her lips perched out to meet his. It lasted only seconds, but it seemed much longer. He released both hands and wrapped them around her torso. She copied his move, resting her head on his shoulder as he hugged her close to him. After a minute, she raised her head and looked into his waiting eyes. There was a small tear in her right eye that glimmered in the moonlit sky.

"Why are you crying? What's wrong?"

"Nothing is wrong. I'm just happy, that's all. When Karen said you were a good kisser… I never knew how great a kiss can be."

"That was your first kiss, wasn't it?"

"Was it that obvious?"

"No, it wasn't. Don't tell Karen I said this, but you are a better kisser than she is."

"Now you're just flirting again…"

"With you, I'm never flirting. You are a better kisser because you are the only one I want to kiss. It was a great kiss because we both were there kissing each other. I couldn't do it without you."

He leaned back into her, and they kissed again. Nothing more was said.

They walked back to the house, where they found Donna's car sitting in the driveway. There was Mr. Fusco sound asleep on his recliner. Donna was in the kitchen, talking to Michelle and Mrs. Fusco, having a piece of apple pie.

"We were about to come out and look for you. Did you two enjoy your walk?" Michelle said, directing the question at her sister. Patti started to blush, and Gary went to her rescue.

"I could walk another two miles and still not work off that dinner. Mrs. Fusco, thanks for inviting me. The food was fantastic."

They all said their goodbyes, and Patti walked Gary and Donna to the car. Donna quickly got into the car, and Gary gave Patti a final kiss for the evening and told her he would see her at church in the morning. He got in the car, put on the seat belt, and Donna proceeded to drive back home.

She had gotten to the end of the block when she couldn't hold back any longer.

"See you at church in the morning? Boy, do you have it bad."

"Shut up and drive. Don't ruin this evening for me."

"Okay, stud. I won't say another word…tonight…but I am calling Aunt Connie in the morning."

CHAPTER 14

As expected, Gary's ankle was well healed by the end of the week. Friday came, and the doctor gave him the okay to play again. He was out running on it by the next morning, and he was going to the beach with Patti that afternoon. Everything turned around really fast in that past week. He got through the week without any more incidences with the gang of bullies. He had gone to JV practice all week long even though he couldn't dress out or anything, but he wanted to keep involved, as Coach Lewis put it. He had looked forward to this weekend because it would allow himself to put away the act and relax more around everyone, especially Patti. He had to be home this Saturday night to watch Carol because his mom was going out on a date. She refused to discuss it with them and was very evasive, even with Donna's continued barrage of questions. Gary was not one to ask a lot of questions; his forte was to watch and listen and come to his own conclusions. It was too early to get involved in his mother's dating life. She had been on dates since his father died, but none had ever been long-term. This might just be a onetime thing, so he wasn't interested. He would not take too much notice unless it got to three dates. Then he would get curious. Tonight, he would be content to hang out in his room online or on the phone with Patti.

He checked online, and most of his friends there must have had things to do other than be there. He got a nasty letter from Kim, who said she saw he was online but ignored her invites to meet her in a chat room. He wrote her a quick email back to apologize and signed off. He had already decided he was going to slow down his online chatting because of Patti. The more time they spent together, even if it was just talking on the phone, was better time spent. It was going to be school, football, and Patti from then on. He had several months before December to come up with some reason to not meet with Kim when she came down here. She only had been talking about it for about six months. First, she said she would be here in September; now it was pushed back to Christmas. With Patti in the picture, it was no longer important to him.

He went to check on his sister, informed her that he would be on the phone and did not want to be bothered unless the house was on fire. He grabbed the wireless phone and exited to his room.

Throughout the week, Gary had settled into all his classes and overcame the stress he had had to deal with during the first two weeks. He found most of his classes easy, as was usual with him. Algebra 2, biology, English, and European history were a breeze for him. Physical education (PE) was a no-brainer also, with Coach Lewis as the teacher. His only challenge was his religion class. Going to a public school, he never had to take it as an actual class. He remembered going through his catechism classes growing up, but after his confirmation, he stopped going. The religion class was taught by a young priest by the name of Father Timothy Kovlaski.

Father Tim, as he had everyone call him, tried to reach his students by getting them to participate in scriptures instead of just reading them. He had already informed them that there were no tests except the final. Grading was based fully on class participation. Plainly said, the students must read the Bible sections and be prepared to tell him what they thought. Now, asking Gary what he thought was something that Father Tim was not fully prepared for in his class preparation. During the earlier weeks, Gary was quiet and contained due to his orientation to his new school. Now all that was behind him. By the end of the week, Gary had to spend thirty minutes after class because he wasn't done telling him what he thought, and Father Tim was so intrigued with the discussion he dismissed the class at the bell and sat and listened. Gary, at his young age, had had to endure things that most children hadn't had to deal with yet. His uncle being killed in a car crash at five and his father's death when he was ten were life lessons dealt with early. Gary, being the gifted child, put him in different situations.

Now, when you tried to apply the teachings of the Bible to everything that he had to endure, and adding to Gary's inquisitive perception, there came a lot of questions and answers. Father Tim was ready to give the answers to the questions; after all, that was what he was there for. He wasn't prepared, however, to being able to ask questions and having his new young student provide his own unique answers. He felt at ease talking to Father Tim. He had been through all the first four stages of grief since his father died. His mother set the whole family up with counseling. Denial and anger, he moved past quickly. Bargaining he dismissed because he thought past trying to make a deal with God and he never got depressed over the loss because he believed that his father never really left him. Of course, physically he did, but his father taught him so much about overcoming his negatives and making things positive that he always felt him there with him. With that, he never got to the fifth and final stage, acceptance. The poem he gave to Kim during the summer was the one he wrote during his counseling sessions. He showed Father Tim his poem and talked about his father. He told him of his father's plan to send him to this school and all the hard changes his family had had to do to follow it.

Father Tim finally got the chance to ask him a question that put Gary silent for a moment.

"Gary, do you still have those moments like in the poem when you are in darkness and scared?"

Gary thought about the question. Did he? He never thought about it. Especially lately. With all the changes, he was too involved to notice or think about it. But then he did realize that he indeed had moments of fear and didn't realize it. The day Lynda dumped him and left for vacation. The day they got the letter about his acceptance to SCC was another one. Going out for the football team at his new school and having to tackle Jimmy. Getting beaten up on the first day of school and then finding out he couldn't play football because of transfer rules. There were moments of fear after all those.

"Yes, I guess I do, but I get by them knowing I can handle it somehow."

"How do you handle it?"

"Like I always have. If I don't know the answer, I just ask my father. I'm never alone. Alive or dead, he is always with me."

"Do you talk to your father a lot?"

"Not a lot, just at times. When I was younger, my dad and I would talk, and it would just get me thinking about stuff. After he died, I missed not having him here to help me with my thought process."

"So your poem is your way of having your father still be here with you. That's interesting, Gary. When you say you are 'looking into the heavens,' what do you consider the heavens?"

"The space between my mind and my soul, the parts of me that only I can see and feel. A place where I can overcome my fears and gain strength and guidance. It's where my dad will be to help me through it all."

"Do you feel that 'looking into the heavens' will get you the guidance to get through the rest of your life?"

"Yes. I will always be looking into the heavens because I know he will always be there, looking down on me."

"Gary, you may not believe it, but with you agreeing to come to this school as your father planned, and that last statement, you had accepted your father's death. I wish I could have met him, but in a way, I think I just did. The best parts of your father are alive inside of you. Don't ever lose sight of that."

"I won't. Thanks for the talk, Father, but I have to get to practice."

"Go, then, and thank you, Gary. You did most of the talking. I just listened. Anytime you need to talk and your father is out playing golf with Jesus, stop in and see me."

Gary laughed at the joke, grabbed his books, and left for practice. He had some catching up to do on the team, and their first game was in two days. The JV team didn't really have another kicker. The punter was also kicking field goals in practice while he was out, but Gary was better than him. Practice was another hot one, but no more than he was used to.

Two hours later, the boys dragged themselves into the locker room. JV practice was thirty minutes shorter than for the varsity so that the two teams didn't compete for shower space. He quickly showered, dressed, and left for the parking lot. Donna didn't like to be kept waiting. To his surprise, his sister wasn't there, but in her stead, his mother was waiting at the car, talking to Sister Jean. He just got hit with one of those fear moments that he had talked to Father Tim about earlier. He approached the car quietly, anticipating the worst.

"There's my little brainiac now."

"Hi, Sister Jean. Am I in trouble or something?"

"No, Gary. I was just telling your mother that if I don't keep you in check, you will start doing my job soon. Like I said, he already is tutoring his friends at lunch period. Yesterday he had about eight students with books open at the lunch table, going over homework for my class."

"The work is easy, Sister, and I can't tell them no."

"It's okay. Just teach, don't do it for them. That's all I ask."

"No problem. Mom, what are you doing here? Where's Donna?"

"I just got home early, and I wanted to pick you up. Get in the car. We have to get home. It was nice to meet you, Sister."

They all said their goodbyes and got in the car to leave. He noticed his mother looking back in the mirror but decided not to pry.

The ride home was quiet. As usual, Gary was deep in thought. He always enjoyed the ride home after football practices. It gave his body a chance to relax after dealing with the heat and humidity of the late South Florida afternoons. He adjusted the car's air-conditioning vent to blow air directly at his face and started to plan out his evening. He scheduled in his mind the order he would do his homework after supper. There was nothing on television that he wanted to watch, so he decided to plan on checking up what was happening in the chat rooms for a bit. He had been good to his commitment to be less involved online, but he already knew that Patti and her family were not going to be home tonight, so that left an opening in his evening that had to be filled.

They arrived home, and Gary drudged into the house, carrying his gym bag and books.

After he finished his homework, Gary went to the kitchen for a snack. Carol had possession of the television, which was fine with him. Donna was in the kitchen, talking on the housephone with Steve. His mom was nowhere to be found.

"Where's Mom at?" he asked Donna, who was annoyed by his interruption.

"She's in her room, talking to her new boyfriend on her cell."

He was a bit shocked at his sister's open reference to his mother having a "boyfriend." He decided that he needed to find out more information about it.

"Who's her new boyfriend? Did you get a name yet?"

"No, and I'm on the phone with my boyfriend right now, and his name is Steve. Take your Oreos and milk and leave me alone."

He was not in the mood to argue with his sister, so he let the issue go and complied with her demand. An argument was not part of his schedule tonight, so he went back to his room, set his snack on his desk, and sat down at his computer to find his online friends. He decided to check his email and found he had one each from Lisa and Kim. The letter from Lisa was very short and surprising. She said that her father had restricted her from talking online for a month and, after that, with anyone whom she didn't go to school with. This meant that she would no longer be able to talk to him and this was goodbye. Kim's letter was close to the same; however, her parents were only punishing her for three weeks, but she would still be able to talk to him after that. This was way too much drama for Gary right now, especially from two people he had never met. This just confirmed his decision to break off his online friendships and use his time with his real-life friends.

He found Mike in one of his regular chat rooms and was content to talk to him for the rest of the evening.

CHAPTER 15

The last two weeks finished better than the first two weeks of his new school year, but Gary finished his first full month and was very happy at his accomplishments. The JV team was 2–0, and he had played to his full potential at his position. His next game was Wednesday and against his old school, and Gary was at odds on how he was going to handle going down there to play against his friends there. He did his best to try not to think about it, but his plans for Saturday didn't help.

The last weekend of September was the last chance to surf any decent waves in South Florida. Steve had planned an outing at Haulover Beach with Donna. Gary jumped at the opportunity to work at getting invited. What started out as just Steve and Donna going alone escalated to a whole group. Gary, of course, invited Patti, who couldn't go to Miami Beach unless her sister Michelle went along. Then Frank and Barbara got included, so with Barbara and Michelle going, Karen couldn't be excluded. With everyone else going, his mom, Aunt Connie, and Carol decided to make the party bigger and join in. Mike was invited at the last minute, so needless to say, they had a caravan of cars driving down to Miami Beach. Gary thought it best not to mention to Steve that he had talked to Manny, who was also going to meet them there with his family. He was happy enough, though, when he was told that Jimmy would not be part of the group. Gary made a mental note to keep football off the topic of conversation with Manny. He didn't want to start any rivalry now that he was playing against him next week. With all the cars packed with people, towels, sunscreen, food, and surfboards, they set off at seven thirty to make their track down south.

Haulover Beach was about the best surfing beach in South Florida. Depending on the weather, you could almost surf anywhere if you weren't particular about the size of the waves. With the hurricane season winding down, the opportunities of getting bigger waves were soon to be scarce. If it were up to Gary and Steve, they would have been out at the beach by seven thirty instead of leaving the house to make the two-hour track to get down there. Manny and his family were already there, and Manny himself was already in the water. The boys took advantage of the girls by grabbing their boards and rushing to the ocean, leaving them to unload everything.

After about an hour, Gary made it back to the group and invited Patti out for more "lessons" on his board. When they made it out to where Manny was floating, Gary made a quick introduction to Patti to his old friend. He undid his board leash from his ankle and put it on Patti's, slid off the board, and swam over to Manny's board to hang on to.

"She's all yours. Get ready. Here comes a good wave for you."

Patti looked at him with a stern look because she could tell he was showing off in front of his friend. She decided, though, she was going to show him that she could do it and lay down quickly on the board and started to paddle. She caught the wave perfectly, and it started to take her. She pushed up with her arms and got to her feet as fast as she could and took the wave about a third of the way into the shore before she lost her balance and fell off. She climbed back on the board and started to paddle back out to Gary. When she got close, he swam over to her and started to climb onto the board but quickly found himself back in the water after Patti pushed him back in.

"Hey, what did you do that for?"

"You surfed for an hour by yourself while you left me on the beach. You can watch me for a while."

Manny was laughing uncontrollably at how she put him in his place. Gary couldn't get mad at either of them, so he managed to give back a smile to her response. Patti just looked back, saw another wave starting to form, and started to paddle to catch it. She was well on her way when Manny stopped laughing and looked down to his friend.

"Gary, I like her. You finally found a girl that could control you. Get on. Take me back to shore and you can use my board for a while until she gives you yours back."

Gary climbed on the front of the board, and they caught the next wave back in. He then paddled back out to Patti, who was waiting for him to return. As he approached her, he noticed a stoic look on her face.

"Are you mad at me for pushing you and taking your board?"

"Not at all. You will pay for it sometime in the near future, but right now, you're safe."

"Oh, really? And how am I going to pay for it?"

"I haven't figured that out just yet, but you will know when I do."

"Oh, the quick-thinking, intelligent, overachieving Gary Moran hasn't figured something out yet? Is salt water like kryptonite to you? Did I just figure out your weakness that makes you like the rest of us?" She started to smile at him to let him know she was just having some fun with him.

Gary maneuvered his board next to her and grabbed her hand and pulled her and the board closer to him. He leaned over and gave her a slow, passionate kiss and then pushed her away.

"Did you like that?" he asked.

"Yes, thank you."

"Good. Your punishment is that you won't get another one of those until you ride that board all the way in."

"That's just mean. You may never kiss me again."

She reached out and grabbed Gary's arm and pulled him back close before he could react. Without warning, she pushed him hard off the board and back into the water. "If you are going to punish me like that, pushing you in a second time can't hurt me any worse."

She quickly paddled to catch the next wave, and Gary was quick back up on his board to follow. She got to her feet and fought to maintain her balance as she made her way to shore. He was sure she was going to fall and he would be able to catch up with her, but she just kept going. To his surprise, and hers as well, she freely jumped off her board in the shallow waters of the shoreline. She did her best to drag the board out of the water, but Manny and Mike had run down and helped the rest of the way. The crowd onshore was cheering to her accomplishment. Gary made it to shore himself, where Manny came over to retrieve his board.

"You're a hell of a teacher, Gary."

"I just know how to motivate her. And for the record, she doesn't control me."

"I don't know. She seemed to have more control on those waves than you did."

Gary ignored the shot his friend just took on his ego.

Patti was standing onshore next to his board, waiting for him to come over. She was smiling as he started over but quickly changed to a grimace as he got closer. He knew she had outdone his "punishment" and he would have to kiss her now. He moved in close to her to do so, but she put her hand on his chest and stopped him.

"No way, Moran! You think you are going to get off with one kiss here in front of everyone to save your pride? Later, when we are alone, I will tell you when and how many." She started to smile and then walked back up to the beach. He picked up his board and started up the beach, only to notice Patti getting high fives from everyone. He was even more surprised when he saw Donna whispering something in Patti's ear.

Great. That's all I need is Donna coaching my girlfriend, he thought to himself.

Everyone was having a great time. Manny told them that his cousin was supposed to be by around one o'clock. Gary knew almost all the Herta family who were scattered around South Florida. They would have filled the beach if all of them came. He had been to many of their family get-togethers and learned to love the Cuban cuisine that was in abundance at them.

After lunch, Gary asked Patti to take a walk to the marina. After getting his mother's permission, they walked down Collins Avenue together, talking about their morning confrontation and laughing off the consequences. All was fine between them. Gary was even looking forward to finding out just how many kisses she wanted from him later.

They arrived at the docks just in time for the morning fishing charters returning with their catches. Patti had her camera and was snapping pictures of the boats, the fishermen, and their fish. When they got to the main sign in front of the marina, Gary insisted on taking a picture of Patti standing next to the sign. As he was focusing in on her, he noticed three people exiting a small fishing boat and thought he recognized the woman in the group. He took a couple of pictures of Patti and then got another person to take a picture of both of them together. As they started to walk back to the beach, it started to irk Gary that he couldn't remember where he had seen that woman before. Still holding Patti's camera, he stopped and turned around just in time as the three people reached the street and were standing there, talking. He quickly took a picture of them, focusing on the woman in the center of his lens. He turned back again, took Patti's hand, and continued back to the beach.

"What was that all about?"

"Nothing. That woman looks familiar, and I can't figure out where I know her from."

"Wow, Gary, that was twice in one day you had trouble 'figuring' something out. No more salt water for you."

"Yes, I'm feeling kinda weak. Maybe I need a kiss to counteract the salt water."

"Nice try. I will kiss you when I want to, not when *you* want to."

"That's okay. Good thing Karen is here. Maybe she can cure me."

"Hmm, better start figuring if that cure has any adverse side effects…or is the salt water going to stop your figuring again and get you in more trouble?"

"I was only kidding. I will die before I allow another girl to touch these lips."

"See, standing in this sun is evaporating the salt water from your skin. You're thinking again, so you are cured, and you don't need any kisses at all from anyone."

They made it back to the beach in time to see everyone packing up all the blankets, umbrellas, and beach chairs. His mom and aunt had had it with the heat and salt air and were calling it a day. Gary wanted to go back out to surf, but the waves had died down since the morning, so he surrendered to the idea of leaving and went to get his board. Manny and his family were going to stay a little longer, waiting for his cousin to arrive. He said goodbye to his friend and told him he would see him at the game on Wednesday.

After all the cars were loaded, they started their trip back to Palm Beach County. Gary got stuck in the middle of the back seat of his mom's car between Patti and Carol. With his mom and aunt in the front seat and his little sister in the back, it was not an ideal alone time with Patti as he had hoped. He made the best of it, however, by getting Patti invited over for dinner that evening, so he would be able to spend the rest of the afternoon with her, anyway.

When they arrived back at the house, they informed Michelle of the invite, which Donna quickly extended to her as well. Donna and Michelle had formed their own friendship over the past couple of weeks, to Gary's dismay. Just what he didn't need, his sister providing intel about him to his girlfriend through her sister. He made a mental note to discuss this with Donna as soon as he could.

They had two hours before dinner to spend more time together. Patti suggested that he show her his computer and the chat rooms he talked in. He was hesitant at first but then remembered that Kim and Lisa were on punishment and wouldn't be online for a couple of weeks. Barring the remote chance of running into Lynda, he felt it would be safe to show her his internet world. They hooked up her camera to the computer and picked the photos to keep and the ones to delete. Gary downloaded all the pictures he wanted to keep into a folder. He did his best to show her all the features of his computer, although it was difficult to do so with all the noise filtering in from the kitchen. He started to rethink his choice of rooms under these circumstances but soon realized that the noise had stopped, and he got up to see why. He walked through the kitchen and into the living room, and there was no one there. He called out for his mother but got no answer. Before he could call out again, he heard a door open and saw Carol walking down the hallway.

"Mom is in the shower, Donna and Michelle went to the store, and I'm trying to take a nap, so shut up and quit yelling." She turned and walked back to her bedroom.

Gary walked back to his bedroom, where Patti was still sitting at his computer, looking at the pictures that they took. He informed her of the reason for the sudden silence, and she got up and walked over to him. She put her arms around his neck and pulled his lips to hers. It had always been Gary who initiated any romantic advances, but today Patti was taking the lead. As she broke off the kiss, she opened her eyes and looked directly into his, still with her arms around him.

"Don't you ever tell me you aren't going to kiss me anymore to punish me," she said with tears forming in her eyes.

"Never again." He wiped the tears with his finger and held her in his arms. Sitting down on his desk chair, she climbed comfortably into his lap. They cuddled and kissed there until they heard the front door open. Quickly they scrambled to their feet and turned their attention to the computer screen. Donna peeked in and told them they were back.

"Kind of quiet in here, Gary?" She turned back to Michelle. "He's such a Boy Scout."

Gary and Patti both ignored the comments and just spent the rest of the time together while waiting for dinner to be served. They had all had a good day today, and his sister was not going to spoil it for them.

CHAPTER 16

The JV team left the school at one thirty to make the trip down to South Miami for the four o'clock game with South Kendall High School. Gary was doing the best he could trying to relax and prepare himself for the game. He was worried about running into Mr. Browning and what might be said about him playing in the game today. Coach Lewis was traveling with the team today if there was a problem. It was very unusual that he would take the time off away from the varsity team's practice to go watch the JV play at an away game, but he was also concerned that there might be a problem. Even Gary's mother, who was down in Miami, anyway, was going to be at the game.

They arrived at the field and assembled at the far side to put on their shoulder pads and jerseys and warm up for the game.

As the team ran over to their sidelines, Gary noticed Mr. Browning in the stands. He turned quickly to just ignore him but turned back thirty seconds later only to notice that he wasn't looking his way. Gary was chosen as one of the cocaptains and went out to the center of the field to handle the coin flip. They had won the toss and elected to receive the kickoff; he quickly shook hands with his former teammates and ran back to the bench for the start of the game.

The game went off without any problems. He overcame his anxiety and settled into playing the game with determination and conviction and made both his extra points after the touchdowns his team scored. He had no opportunity at any field goals because their offense was really being manhandled by his former team. The game ended with them losing 24–14. It was a disappointing loss, but on that day, they were not the better team. He went over to shake hands with the opposing team and to look for his friend Manny. He had looked for him on the opposite sidelines throughout the game but did not see him. As he approached two boys he had known from last year, he asked where his friend was.

"Manny didn't come to school today. Didn't you hear about his cousin?"

"No. I didn't. Which cousin? What happened?"

"His cousin Carlos. He had been missing since Saturday, and they found him dead last night."

Gary was stunned. He became dizzy and confused and fell to his knees, driving his helmet into the ground, and started to cry. As both teams started to crowd around him, Coach Parr, who had reached him before any of the other coaches, moved the crowd back and helped him to his feet. Gary could not contain himself as his coach did his best to console him. By the time they got back to the bench, Gary's mother, Coach Lewis, and Mr. Browning were there to meet them. Gary saw his mother, dropped his helmet, and fell into her arms. He began to cry again.

"Mr. Browning just told me about Carlos, honey. I'm so sorry." She held her son tight as any mother would when her child was hurting. It was a pain that unfortunately she was too familiar with. Manny was like a brother to him, and he was so close with the Herta family he held a close connection to them. It took several minutes, but Gary finally composed himself and got some control of his emotions. He stepped away from his mother, closed his eyes for a quick moment, then looked up but said nothing. He looked around and saw that the team was already walking toward the bus.

"Mom, I need to go see Manny." He slid off his shoulder pads and jersey and handed them to Coach Lewis. "Coach, I need to go see my friend. Can my mom take me from here instead of going back on the bus?"

"You go do what you have to do. Marie, he's all yours," Coach Lewis responded.

"Thank you, Charles. Let's go, Gary. Let's go see Manny." She put her arm around her son, but he shrugged it off. He was done crying and no longer needed the support at that moment. He started to go into thought mode.

His friend Carlos was found dead last night but had been missing since Saturday. He needed to know what happened, and he needed to know why. His first concern was for Manny. Manny and Carlos were close. They were the same age and, up to a year ago, had lived blocks apart from each other all their lives. Growing up, it was always the three of them caravanning the neighborhood on their bikes. Carlos's father hit the lottery almost a year ago, and they moved into a house on Miami Beach. They only lived about a mile from the beach they were at on Saturday; that was why it would have been easy for Carlos to meet them there. He speculated that Carlos never did show up on Saturday, but if he didn't, why didn't Manny call him to tell him he didn't? Too many questions.

They got to his mother's car; he climbed into the front seat and remained quiet during the ride to the Herta residence. His mother was already on the phone to Donna to tell her what happened and that they would be late getting home.

When they arrived, there were several cars parked in the driveway, the grass, and on the street. There were also two Metro-Dade police cars parked in the street, with three news crews' vans parked a couple of houses away. Gary's mom pulled into a driveway of a neighbor whom she had known, and after exchanging pleasantries, they started to walk down to the Hertas' house. They were stopped from entering the property by a uniformed officer, but Manny's sister had seen Gary from the living room window and Mr. Herta came out to the house and got the officer to let them in.

The house was filled with family, some talking Spanish, some English, some a little of both. Gary didn't see Manny right off, so he just walked back to his bedroom like he lived there. The door was closed, so he knocked. After several attempts, he finally just turned the doorknob and it was unlocked. He opened the door and looked inside to find Manny was lying facedown in his pillow, where he apparently had cried himself to sleep. Gary called softly out Manny's name and walked over to the bed and stood there waiting for his friend to wake up. Manny turned over and, with red eyes slowly opening, saw his friend and rolled into a sitting position. As he tried to stand, Gary stopped him and told him to stay seated. He knew at this point he needed to stay strong for his friend. No more crying for him.

"What the fuck happened?" Gary said bluntly. He knew if he put on a strong front, Manny would toughen up also. "How was Carlos killed?"

"He wasn't killed. He was kidnapped, but they didn't kill him. They said there were no signs of trauma on his body."

Gary thought a moment. "They didn't know he was diabetic, I bet. He never showed up on Saturday, did he?"

"No, he didn't. We waited till three and called his house. They said he was meeting someone at eleven. They thought he was meeting us, but when we told my uncle that Carlos said he would be here at one, he called the police. They got the ransom demands the next morning."

"Why didn't you call me?"

"We weren't told about the kidnapping or the ransom till this morning, when they told us they found Carlos's body. What did you mean about them not knowing about him being diabetic?"

"We know Carlos was type 1 and took insulin all his life. How would the kidnapper know that? Carlos never wanted anyone to know. Remember, all through elementary school, he wouldn't let us tell anyone. He didn't want anyone to know that he had to take daily injections. If they took him, fed him, and didn't give him his daily shot, his blood sugar might have shot up and it killed him. No signs of trauma on his body. They will confirm it with the autopsy."

"Gary, you got that look on your face again. What are you thinking about? You aren't going to get involved in this, are you?"

"I'm not going to just let the police try to figure out who killed him. Don't tell anyone about this."

"If you are right, then they didn't kill him. It was an accident."

"No, they took him away from his medicine by force. By doing that, they are responsible for his death, and I'm going to find the bastards before the police do."

"It's not the police you have to worry about. They have an FBI federal task force that's in control of the case. They are over talking to my uncle right now, and we are expecting some of them here this afternoon to take statements from us."

"Why is the FBI involved in a local kidnapping?"

"I don't know. Why wouldn't they get involved?"

"They wouldn't on a local and individual case." Gary paused and thought for a second. "Unless there are other kidnappings that fit this profile."

"Damn, Gary, how do you think about all this?"

"I just do. Let's go check it out on your computer."

They both left the bedroom to make their way to the family room, where the computer was set up. The room was packed with most of the family, and there were some new additions to the group. Four men in dark suits were there; two were in the kitchen, talking to Mr. Herta, and two were in the family room, dismantling the computer. Gary assumed that they were the FBI, and using the Herta computer was not going to be an option at this time. He turned to his friend and whispered in his ear to keep the conversation they had in the room a secret for now. He moved closer to the kitchen to see if he could overhear the questions the agents were asking Mr. Herta. As he stood there, he felt a hand on his shoulder. He turned to see that a fifth agent had entered the house and caught him eavesdropping.

"Can I help you with something, young man?"

"No. Who the hell are you?" Gary responded arrogantly. He was still upset inside and lost any control of being polite.

"Special Agent James Kelly, FBI, and your name is?"

"Gary Moran. Manny Herta is my best friend. Are you here to catch the people who killed Carlos?"

"That's the plan. Is your father here somewhere?"

"My father died when I was ten. My mom is over there." He waved to his mother to come over.

"Hello, Mrs.... Moran? I'm Special Agent James Kelly. I head up the FBI federal task force in charge of this case. Can I ask Gary a couple of questions?" Without hesitation, she complied with his request. "So, Gary, how well did you know Carlos?"

"We grew up together in the neighborhood, that is, until he moved last year. Do you have any leads yet on who did this?"

"Um, how about you let me ask the questions, okay? When was the last time you saw Carlos?"

"Last Christmas, here at Manny's house. I moved to Palm Beach four months ago, so I haven't seen the whole family for a while now."

"Ever talk to him online?"

"Once in a while, I ran into him in a chat room. Why? Was that how he was picked as a target?"

"Again, with the questions? You want to run my task force, or can I do my job here?" He paused to see if his sarcasm was going to be answered. Gary picked up the intent and decided to back down from his inquisitiveness and let Agent Kelly ask his questions without retort. "Have you ever been in any chat room where he was talking to other teenage girls? Girls who aren't local?"

"Yeah. We talked to a lot of different people, girls and guys. I don't know if he was talking to anyone regularly."

"Can you remember any of the names of the people he talked to in these chat rooms?"

"No. Everyone had different screen names. I don't think we ever talked to the same people."

"Okay, that's all for now." He asked Gary for his address, phone number, and date of birth and then handed him a card. "This is my direct phone number. If you think of anything that can help, please call me."

As he stood there looking at the card, he overheard the agent who had started interviewing Manny. He mentioned a couple of names, and one quickly stood out that caught his attention. He made a mental note and decided that he needed to get back home to check out some information using his computer. His mother at the same time realized that with the agents doing their interviews with the family, they might be in the way, and she told Gary it would be a good time to leave and let them do their job.

Gary waved to Manny to get his attention, motioned that they were leaving, and just yelled out, "Call me later!" They walked back to their car, and Gary climbed in the back seat. He asked his mom if he could use a notepad and pencil from her briefcase. After she gave him her permission, he pulled out the notepad and started to write down all the information that he had compiled that afternoon. He was quiet all the way home, lost in his thought. He drew out a game plan in his head and wrote a list of information he needed to look up. This was by far the most difficult task he had ever undertaken, but for Carlos he was determined to succeed.

CHAPTER 17

Jerry quickly grabbed his suitcase and began to repack all his belongings. The flight he took to Rio was very turbulent, and after the last couple of days he had, it wasn't something he was looking to repeat so soon. He decided that the team was to disperse after the mishap in Florida. He still couldn't believe that the kid just died on them. Everything was going as planned. Everything was perfect, just like all the other times. The kid didn't even look sick, so he was really confused with what went wrong. Lauren bought her ticket and was on the way to meet him in Rio. Manual already had the equipment moved to a new location prior to the abduction and left immediately to go back to Dallas. Eddie dumped the body on a bus bench and headed to Fort Lauderdale Airport to fly out to Atlanta in the middle of the night. By the time the body was discovered, the team was completely out of the state. He was sure they had covered their tracks as they always had in all the previous cases.

He had decided that staying in Rio was not safe. If they decided to check out the bank where he would be at right now physically removing the money and leaving before they could trace the transfer, it would not be wise to be seen and perhaps someone making a connection after the fact. He grabbed his suitcases and checked out.

Lauren would not arrive for another four hours, so he jumped in a taxi and had the driver take him to a car rental center. He drove out to the local marketplaces outside the main city. He did his best to blend in as a tourist buying Brazilian trinkets and savoring the local cuisine. He took the time to backtrack the events of the past three days. The abduction went as he had planned. They arrived at the marina in time to meet up with Eddie when he docked with the target. He was still asleep and bound in the hold of the boat. He would be that way for another two hours. They walked to a nearby restaurant to kill time while the target recovered. They returned in time as he started to recover from his drugged state. They untied him and made him drink ipecac syrup to make him throw up on himself. No one on the dock suspected anything as they walked the boy off the boat, kidding him about getting seasick on his first fishing outing. Eddie called him later to tell him the boy was secured and fully recovered from being drugged. He was scared, but no signs of him being sick in any way. He had left to fly to Rio after the call, and by the time he landed, the boy was dead. Something about the boy he missed. Something everyone missed. He decided he had to go back to find out what. He made it back to his car in time to get to the airport to pick up Lauren.

Lauren was very distraught when she was departing the plane. Jerry picked up on her condition and immediately started damage control. He had already purchased two tickets back to New York for them and knew that he only had less than thirty minutes to calm her down and get her back on the plane for the trip back to the States. He moved her to the nearest bar and got a couple of drinks in her before he told her of the travel plans. She was to take a short flight back home to Vermont as soon as they arrived in New York. He knew she would feel responsible for the boy's death, and he needed her to move past it so he could plan his next move. He knew that sending her home would move her out of the way and give her time to heal. He was going to call his old friend on the FBI as soon as he arrived back in New York and volunteer his services on the federal task force.

CHAPTER 18

It had been a month since the funeral, and everything in Gary's life had returned to a sense of normalcy. The JV season had just finished, and he was enjoying his new school more every day.

The final bell had just rung, and he was making his way to the parking lot when he heard someone calling for him. He turned and saw Coach Parr standing near the boys' locker room. He quickly walked back to his coach to see what he wanted.

"Gary? You weren't at the varsity game last Friday, were you?"

"No, I had some things to do and couldn't make it. I've been down at my friend's house in Miami over the weekend. Just got back home late last night."

"So you haven't heard what happened at the game then…about Jimmy?"

"No, what happened to Jimmy?" Gary felt a moment of gloom come over him with that question. He was just getting adjusted from Carlos's death. He wasn't ready for more bad news about another friend.

"Jimmy tore his ACL during a tackle after a kickoff. He's out for the rest of the season. Coach Lewis wanted me to ask you about playing the last two games on the varsity schedule."

Gary paused, totally unprepared for that proposal. One part of him was screaming yes inside. Playing varsity was what he originally wanted. But after what happened to Carlos, football wasn't really a priority at that time. However, he knew that such a request was something that he couldn't say no to.

"Sure, Coach. I guess that means I have practice this afternoon. My sister should be in the parking lot to pick me up. I have to go find her to tell her that I'm staying. I suppose you already have a practice uniform waiting for me inside?"

"Yeah, I guess we do. We can't put anything over on you, can we?" He smiled, which was something Gary had not seen his coach do all during the JV season.

He went to go find his sister to tell her the news. To his surprise, she was waiting for him with his gym bag with clean clothes, to which he surmised that she had prior knowledge of his good fortune. He didn't have time to question her on what, why, and when she knew something, because he didn't want to be any later to practice than he already would be. He threw his book bag in the car and grabbed his gym bag and ran to practice. She would be back to pick him up; he would interrogate her later.

On the way back to the locker room, he ran into Patti and Michelle and told them about his promotion to varsity. Patti seemed relieved that, as unfortunate as it was for Jimmy to get hurt, it was what she knew Gary needed. He had been very distant that last month, and she knew this would help him redirect his thoughts past his friend's death.

Gary hurried to get dressed and rush out of the locker room with a purpose.

As he approached the field, he noticed practice had already started and Jimmy was on crutches on the sideline. As he neared, Jimmy waved him over to him.

"Well, Gary, I guess you have to finish this for me."

"Yeah, I guess so. How bad is the knee?"

"I'm scheduled for more tests tomorrow, and probably surgery on Friday. Then we just see how it heals in time."

"That sucks. Is this going to hurt your scholarship chances?"

"Not yet. My dad talked to the Florida State scout today, who says they will see how I heal before making any decisions. You better get out there. Lewis is looking at you."

"Yeah, I see him. I gotta go. Good luck on the surgery."

Gary put on his helmet and ran to his coach, who directed him to stretch and warm up. He worked hard at practice to show he really belonged here. This was what he wanted in the first place, and now he was there. Regardless of how he got there, he was motivated to prove himself to his coaches and new teammates.

By the end of practice, he had back the stamina that he had the month earlier at the end of the JV season. He took a quick shower and dressed to go home. He made it out to the parking lot, where he saw his mother talking to Coach Lewis.

"There's my little man now," his mom said as he approached. He really hated when she said that, and his expression showed it. He blew off the comment, however, as he didn't want to show his displeasure in front of his coach.

"Thanks for giving me the opportunity to play on the varsity team, Coach."

"You earned the chance, Gary. You had a good season on the JV team, and unfortunately with Taylor getting hurt, we are just lucky that we have you to step up and fill the void."

"I won't let you down. Mom, what happened to Donna? I thought she was going to pick me up?"

"She had other things to do, so I decided to pick you up instead. Get in. I'm betting you are hungry after the practice you had."

Gary climbed into the car and buckled himself in the seat. He was quiet as they drove out of the parking lot and said nothing for most of the drive home. His mother was curious about his demeanor but decided not to question him about it. It was Gary who was the first to talk as they arrived at the house, and she shut the car off.

"Mom, how is it going between you and Coach Lewis? You two have been dating for over two months now."

"What? How did you know?" She paused to consider an answer to her own question. "I should have known we couldn't put anything over on you. When did you know?"

"I suspected for a time now, but when Donna showed up with my gym bag and you showed up to pick me up, it was something that kind of confirmed it."

"Okay, so now you know. Are you okay with it?"

"I don't know yet. I have to think about it more."

"Well, you think about it, but don't go telling all your friends about it. We don't want people to get the idea you have any special privileges at the school."

"Yeah, neither do I. Besides, with Coach Lewis, he works me harder than anyone else on the team. I guess he is overcompensating because of you. Thanks, Mom."

"You know you can handle it, so don't start whining now. Let's go in before dinner gets cold."

They went into the house, and Gary went straight to his room to drop off his books and notes from today, so he could start on his homework right after dinner. With everything else he had going on, now he had to deal with his mother and coach dating each other. He figured he would work it all out tonight and, like always, added a mental note to his internal schedule to handle it.

After dinner, he finished his homework in record time and made his phone call to Patti to tell her about his practice but left out his discovery of his mother's boyfriend. He had to keep his conversation short to keep on his schedule.

He signed into his computer and started to cruise his usual chat rooms. At nine o'clock, he stopped his search for the night. Another night with no results. He would try again tomorrow, like he had been doing for the last month. He was sure she was going to show up eventually. He had to stay on schedule.

He shut down his computer, stripped down to his underwear, shut off the lights, and climbed into bed. His thoughts drifted back and forth. He thought about Carlos, about what happened to him. It troubled him that he was close to the truth but worried what to do with it when he found all of it. He had to focus on everything. He couldn't get any help from anyone. He didn't want to get anyone else involved on his plan. The idea of his mother dating his coach was a new wave of change that he wasn't sure was a good or bad change for him. For his mother, she had seemed happy for the last month, and he suspected that her new relationship with Coach Lewis had a lot to do with it, so for her, it was a good thing, and for that he was happy for it. For Gary, it was a distraction. He closed his eyes and started to think of his father. His father was the only one who could help him.

He was the only one he would trust. Of course, his conversation was just a means to focus on his problems and ease his confusion. The memory of his father relaxed him enough to put aside the conflicts, and soon he was asleep. Tomorrow he would start again.

CHAPTER 19

The weather was getting cooler in Georgia, as it usually did in November. Although it was not quite sweater weather, Jerry was dressed casually in khakis and sweater vest as he left the Atlanta office of the FBI. He had just spent the last two hours in an informal chat with Agent Kelly. He was able to find out about the cause of death of Carlos Herta. It was a careless oversight on his part as to disregard a possible health risk of his target. It was good to find out that the task force had a certain respect for the kidnapping team that they were investigating. Kelly had told him that they were impressed with how he was always two steps ahead of them on every case. He had to really hold back when his friend told him that "the leader of this group was a genius for the planning and execution of each kidnapping." How surprised he would be to find out that "genius" was sitting right in front of him the whole time. He was offered a position on the task force as a consultant but decided that he already got his answers, and declined. He used the excuse that he had to get back to his job as an investigator for a major law firm in Boston that he made more money at than the consultant job he was being offered. He thanked his friend and said goodbye.

He made a call to Eddie, who was waiting nearby with a car to pick him up. After filling Eddie in on the outcome of his meeting, he called the rest of the team and laid out his plans. He had decided that the task force was unprepared for another job right now. In fact, they had figured that their kidnappers would probably lie low because of the death of their last target, and maybe not even attempt another one for quite a while. Jerry had decided that now was the time to hit his last target and retire then as planned. His last call was to Lauren.

Sending her home was a good move, as she had recovered from the last project.

"Okay, Lauren, get packed up and I will have a plane ticket for you to fly back down to Florida tomorrow."

"I don't know, Jerry. You think it's a good idea to try again so soon?"

"It's a great idea. Eddie and I will be flying out this afternoon. Manny will be there in the morning to start setting up the equipment. I need you there so that you can reconnect with the target."

"I don't know if I can…after what happened to Carlos… I… don't want to get anyone else…hurt."

"Come on, baby girl, don't go beating yourself up. He was diabetic. You didn't know. His death was an accident. We can't do this without you."

"Okay, I'll be there, but we will have to make sure nothing happens to Gary."

"We will, I promise. And…uh, Lauren…stop calling the targets by their names. It's not Carlos or Gary. Just say 'the target.' We talked about this before. You call them by their names, you personalize them, and you start seeing them as more than what they are. They are just the targets of the project."

"Okay, fine, sorry. Jerry, I miss you. Are you going to pick me up at the airport?"

"You know I will, baby. I miss you too. Why do you think I am flying you out tomorrow? It's going to take Manny a day or two to get everything set up for you. We are going to take some personal time together."

"I can really use it right now. I've been so stressed out sitting up here, waiting. But, Jerry, please, no beach this trip."

"You got it. We're staying in Fort Lauderdale this time, but I will book a hotel away from the ocean. Maybe we will do some gambling at the Hard Rock."

"You know how much I love blackjack!" Her disposition had done a complete turnaround. He had accomplished his attempt at preparing her for the next and final phase of his plan.

CHAPTER 20

SOUTH CENTRAL CATHOLIC ADVANCE TO FLORIDA 3A DIVISION PLAYOFFS—it was the headline of the sports section of the *Palm Beach Post*. This was the first time the school had ever been in postseason play, and it became the talk around the school. Gary was perfect in his play in the final two games, having made all six extra points and two field goals.

Although the success had the school's attention, it was not the primary train of thought for him. He went to school every day, went to practice, and then was right home to go online. After over two months of waiting, yesterday he was emailed by Kim. He had quickly answered her that he would be busy this week with football practice and he would chat with her this weekend. He wanted to talk to her, but not yet. He needed to confirm his suspicions about her and Lisa. It was Lisa's name that he overheard from the FBI agent at Manny's house. How much of a coincidence was it that right before Carlos was kidnapped, Lisa was being punished and no longer would be able to talk online? Lisa disappeared, but Kim was still able to talk. There was a connection between the two incidents. Lisa was another persona to validate Kim as a real teenager. He had done a search that same day he found out about his friend's death about other kidnappings. He found four kidnappings that he was able to tie back to those the federal task force were investigating. All were males between the ages of thirteen and seventeen, all except for Carlos were returned unharmed after they received the ransom, and all were believed to be targeted by the kidnappers from online contacts. The big question was, Why was he having this online friendship with Kim? Unless he was a target himself. His mother had received a ten-million-dollar life insurance after his father's death, so that would indeed make him a viable target.

The one piece of information he had that the FBI did not was the picture he took at the marina. He remembered where he saw the woman before. He saw her a few times at his new church in Riverside. He believed the woman was Kim. He had been going through all the information in his mind, remembering all the past conversations he had had with her. The times she told him that she would be coming down to South Florida and wanted to meet him. She last told him she would be coming down in December. It was now December. After what had happened to Carlos, was he still a target? He had to be. If not him, they wouldn't be caught. If not now and they went into hiding, they would get away with all of it. That would not work in Gary's plan. She, with her two accomplices, were there at the marina the day Carlos died. Carlos was there, probably in one of the boats at the marina, and still alive, and he didn't know it. It was his turn to make them the targets. He had to talk to "Kim" and make it happen.

He deliberately told her about the playoffs he was going to be in this Saturday. They were playing a school in South Miami, and he was hoping that would entice the kidnappers to show up and check him out. He was prepared for them if they did.

Gary walked over to the light switch and flipped it off, turning the room into instant darkness. He lay down on his bed and closed his eyes. Again, he went over his past chats with Kim. He thought about Manny and the Herta family, and he thought about Carlos. He recounted all the information he found about the other kidnappings. There was so much that he knew now that he had missed before, yet there was a lot more that he didn't know but needed to find out. He had to find out who the other two men in the picture were. The one who was doing most of the talking was probably the leader. He looked to be in his forties and walked straight and forcefully, like a solder in the military. The other was a bit younger and bigger, towering over the others by about five inches. Kim was a petite woman in her very early twenties. She did look young standing next to the others, but she looked at the leader with a more mature look. He remembered at one point that she reached out and took his hand. He remembered it because it was at the same time he had taken Patti's hand as they turned and walked away.

He opened his eyes and peered into the darkness. There was a stillness in the room which allowed his mind to think. There in his mind he saw the brains, the brawn, and the bait in the picture, but there was someone missing—the tech! For them to pull this off, they needed someone who had the knowledge and experience with computers to make the online connections without being caught. There was more information that he needed before he could proceed with his plan.

He jumped out of bed and turned on his computer. It booted quickly, the light from the monitor filling the room with an eerie haze. He proceeded with his search for information for the next three hours, until his mother knocked on his door to tell him it was time he went to sleep.

Marie had some concerns for her son. He had been through a rough time in the last four months. She knew the move was what started all his changes, but unlike other children who would struggle to adapt, Gary was not showing any signs of such of a struggle. If anything, it was the opposite. His demeanor was one of conviction and direction. Instead of being in a depressed state, he moved and acted around the house with an upbeat attitude, like one who had taken on the mountain but had already made it to the top and was waiting for others to arrive so he could tell them of what he had done. He had a reputation for scheming and conniving to accomplish his goals, but in the past, they were all short-term. Now he had been at this for weeks. She knew she couldn't help him; he was too much like his father. Whatever he was working on, he was on his own for now. All she could do was stand back and prepare to catch him if he fell. It was at times like this she wished his father were here to help him. She had been seeing Charles Lewis for three months now, their relationship having gotten stronger since Carlos's death. She leaned on him for her support but was not sure Gary was ready for a new father figure around to do the same. The coach was just that at school to all the students; Gary was no exception, but he was not favored in anyway either. She was prepared to ask him to talk to her son and find out what was on his mind but didn't want to put him into a position that he would be uncomfortable with.

Gary wasn't alone in his task. It was true that he could not trust anyone with what he was working on—at least not yet. He was offered grief consoling at school, but he refused any of it. He did find some solace in his talks with Father Tim, who he trusted more than he did most of his teachers. Father Tim always seemed to be able to listen to Gary and had a good understanding of his complexity. The talks usually started and finished with Gary talking about his father. It made him realize that even though he was undertaking this "project" in finding Carlos's killers by himself, he really wasn't alone in it. He had figured that perhaps he might need some help in his quest, but not so much as to jeopardize anyone else. His plan had risks, but it could only be his risk, not anyone else's. He could not tell Father Tim his plans, or any other teacher or coach. They would just try to stop him. He had to establish contact back with Kim first. She was the key to putting his plan to work.

He got home from practice on Monday afternoon, ate dinner quickly, and went online to continue his research. After about thirty minutes, he got a message from Kim to meet her in a private chatroom.

> **Chickee89:** *Hey you, it's been a while, how have you been.*
> **Pkicker:** *I'm doing ok. I just got home an hour ago. We had a long practice today. Big game is on Friday.*
> **Chickee89:** *Yeah, I got your message. You got moved up to Varsity. Nice going.*
> **Pkicker:** *I sent a new pic of me earlier to your email. It's one of me and Mike in our JV uniforms. I tried sending it to Lisa, but it came back as un-de-liverable. Did her dad delete her account?*
> **Chickee89:** *I think he did. She moved to Boston two months ago, so I haven't even heard from her. And yes, I got your picture. Mike is cute.*

Pkicker: I think you think all guys are cute. Hey, are you still coming down to Miami this month?
Chickee89: Yeah, we will be there the 22nd. You still want to meet me even though you have a girl-friend now?
Pkicker: No girlfriend anymore. We broke up so it's safe for me to meet you.
Chickee89: No girlfriend? What happened? I want details.
Pkicker: It's a long story. I will tell you when I see you. Hey, when am I going to get a pic of you? Soccer season is over. Doesn't your school take pictures?
Chickee89: Yeah, I have one in my soccer uniform.
Pkicker: You owe me. I got you a pic of Mike!! LOL Send it now!!
Chickee89: I will send it if you promise to delete it after you see it. I don't want my picture to be resent to all your other online friends.
Pkicker: I will never do that. You don't do that with my pics, do you?
Chickee89: No, I delete them right after I look at them. My dad checks my hard drive for pictures, so I don't keep any that anyone sends me. I want to keep my computer.
Pkicker: Good idea. You send me your pic and I will promise to memorize what you look like and delete it right after. LOL
Pkicker: Unless you are ugly and then I will just delete it without memorizing it. LOL
Chickee89: Moran, you are such an asshole. Ok, I will send you my pic. Hold on.

Gary hoped he had played his hand well and waited for the computer to tell him that he had mail. There was a good chance that the picture would be of some other girl's picture she pulled off the internet, but he was hoping that he had pushed the right buttons that made her unaware of his true intent. Within three minutes, he received an email from Kim with the picture attachment. He opened the attachment to see a group picture of a girls' soccer team. He scanned the picture and found the girl who looked like the woman he saw at the marina. Just then, he noticed that Kim was back online in the chatroom, messaging him.

> **Chickee89:** *Did you get the picture?*
> **Pkicker:** *Yeah, which one is you?*
> **Chickee89:** *I'm on the top row, that's all I'm telling you.* LOL *You have to just figure it out. Do it quickly and delete the picture.*
> **Pkicker:** *Ok, I memorized all the good-looking ones and just deleted the pic. If you are one on the ugly ones on the team, I will not recognize you when we meet in a couple of weeks.*
> **Chickee89:** *There are no ugly girls on my soccer team. You are an asshole. I really want to meet you now just to hit you.*
> **Pkicker:** *You won't hit me. I'm not scared of you.*
> LOL

Gary continued the conversation for the next half hour. They talked about school and friends and her upcoming Christmas vacation. He knew that everything she told him was a lie. But he went along with the ruse and did his fair share of fabrication of the truth from his end. He had what he needed to continue with his plan.

After she said goodbye, he copied the text of the conversation to a new directory along with her picture. He signed off, shut down his computer, and went to bed. He lay awake for an hour, going over his plan. He felt more confident now that he had verified that he knew the information he had been working on was valid.

CHAPTER 21

Friday night had finally arrived, and Gary was on the bus with the team making it down to South Miami for the game. He had so much on his mind, and the game was not the most important thing he was thinking about. There was a lot that he needed to know at the end of the night which would dictate his plans for the weekend. He took out the picture of Manny, Carlos, and himself when they were all younger. He stared at it for a moment and then slid the picture back into his helmet. It made him sad again remembering how his friend died; however, he turned it back to anger, which he planned on using during the game. Revenge was not normally the method that he used in his scheming, but today, it would do. As they arrived at the stadium, he exited the bus and turned his attention back to game preparation.

In the stands, Gary had several fans who made the trip to see him play. His mom and sisters, of course, Steve, and even Aunt Connie were there to watch him play. The entire Herta family was there, which took a small section of the stands' seating. As he scanned the stands, he saw the Taylor family; Mr. Taylor, with his size, stuck out in a crowd. And of course there were Patti and her parents. Patti was wearing his practice jersey, with the number 11 proudly displayed. He was curious why she offered to wash it for him and demanded that he give it to her to do so. It made him smile at a time he was trying not to. He grabbed a couple of footballs and a kicking tee to loosen up and get some kicking warm-ups before the game started.

Carol went out to the opponents' stands to find Jenny, who said she was going to the game. Also, to find any old friends that she left behind when they moved. As she was walking through the stands, scanning the crowds to find someone she knew, she heard her name being called behind her. She turned to see Lynda racing up the stands to catch up with her.

"Hey, Carol! Who are you looking for?" she said as she got to her. Her camera was dangling around her neck.

"Nobody you would know. What the hell are you doing here?" Carol responded with disdain.

"I'm taking pictures for the school newspaper and yearbook." She moved closer and whispered in Carol's ear, "Also, I am doing a special assignment for Gary."

"What special assignment?" Carol blurted out and was quickly silenced by Lynda before she could finish her sentence.

Lynda whispered back, "I can't tell you. Gary didn't tell me everything, just told me to take pictures of people watching the game. That's all. I've got to go."

Carol watched Lynda as she walked away, stopping at times to take pictures as she went. She thought it was strange that Gary had called her to take pictures during the game. She put it out of her mind, however, as she finally caught a glimpse of Jenny and called to her friend.

Meanwhile, Jerry and Lauren made it to the top of the stands and found some seats where they got a good view of the crowds. Eddie and Miguel found seats away from the other two as to maintain distance in the crowd.

Jerry leaned over to Lauren and whispered, "So which one is our target?"

Lauren whispered back, "Number 11. He is on the field right now, kicking field goals." Lauren then lost her whisper voice and blurted out, "Wow, did you see that? He made that field goal, right down the middle of the crossbars!"

Jerry grabbed her arm and whispered angrily to her, "We are not here to watch the game. We are here to observe the target. Control yourself or go wait in the car." To Jerry, this was a military operation, and he expected his team to stay on target.

Lauren apologized and kept quiet for the rest of the game.

Meanwhile, Lynda was taking pictures of some friends in the stands and saw this guy grabbing a woman's arm. She looked closely and recognized them from the picture Gary had shown her. She made it to right in front of them and then, talking to a group of teenagers positioned in front of them, asking them to smile for the camera, she took several pictures of the group and slyly moved the camera up to get a clean picture of the two people behind them. She discretely popped the digital storage disc from the camera and slipped it in her pocket and replaced it with a previous one she had filled up earlier. As she made it to the base of the stands, she felt a big hand placed on her shoulder and turn her around and make an attempt to take her camera. Lynda, with her long fingernails, scratched his hand and ran down the stands. She heard him behind her, and as she reached the concessions, there were two uniformed police officers. She ran to them and told them about the guy running behind her who had tried to take her camera. As the man made it to the bottom, he ran directly into the two police officers. They began to question him on what he was trying to do. He explained that he was private security for an important man who was here incognito to watch his nephew play. He said that the girl appeared to have taken pictures of his client and merely wanted the pictures deleted if she took any of him and his daughter. He produced an ID which noted he was a security personal but would not give up his client's name. The police officer looked at the ID and said, "Edward Martin," and then called Lynda over and asked for her camera. She handed her camera to the officer and then handed it to Eddie to look at the pictures. He scanned the backup and did not find any pictures of Jerry and Lauren. He handed the camera back to the officer and turned to Lynda to apologize for scaring her. Lynda took the camera back and proceeded to offer Eddie a sour look, that his apology was not accepted. She asked then if she could leave and made her way back to the stands on the other side of the field.

Still shaken, she looked for the Moran family in the stands. The game had just started, and she had to get the disc to Gary somehow as quickly as possible. She saw Steve heading up from the concession stand and asked to speak to him. She looked over and saw that Eddie had sat back down in the stands on the other side of the field and quickly slid the disc into Steve's hand. She then told him, "Give that to Gary and tell him the name Edward Martin. I'm not sure what this is all about. Give it to Gary and don't tell anybody about this." She walked away scared and took out her cell phone and called her father, who was in town. She went back to find the two officers and stood by close to them until her father showed up and picked her up. After she told him what she had done, he took her home and had both her and her mother pack a bag while he made plane reservations to get them out of South Florida. As a photographer who had started out having been assigned to a newspaper crime reporter, he wasn't sure what she got involved in, but he was not taking any chances with his daughter's life.

As halftime approached, SCC was ahead by three points, thanks to the 32-yard field goal that Gary just kicked. Coach Lewis tried to congratulate him as he came off the field; however, he wasn't very cordial to his coach, as he was still focused with the game attitude he had built up inside himself. He grabbed his tee and ran back onto the field to kick off. He set the ball up on the tee, and as soon as the referee blew the whistle, he ran to the ball and kicked it close to the goal line. The returner caught it and started his run. He was fast and quick and was avoiding tacklers and working to break away from his pursuit. But there was no way he was getting by Gary. Gary collided with him about the 45-yard line and took him to the ground with all his fury intact. He rose from the tackle; however, the returner did not. He lay on the ground screaming in pain. They brought out the stretcher and the doctor on call for the game to discover that Gary's tackle broke the boy's collarbone.

Gary made it back to the bench, where Coach Lewis went over to check on his kicker. As Gary removed his helmet, the coach looked in his eyes and did not recognize the young man that he got to know and admire. The picture fell out of the helmet, and the coach picked it up and looked at it intently and then handed it back to Gary.

"Gary, I know you are hurting, but I can't allow you to play with all this anger. You could have killed that boy. I'm sorry, but the game is over for you."

Gary looked at his coach with nothing to say. Coach Lewis looked up in the stands and saw Marie, whom he motioned over to come down to the field. Father Tim helped the coach get Gary to his feet and walked the boy over to his mother, who climbed over people in the stands to get to her son. She put her arms around her son as he started to cry. Father Tim was standing behind him and leaned over to Gary to tell him, "Look into the heavens, Gary. Look into the heavens and you will find all your answers."

Marie sent Steve to get the car as they walked Gary back to the locker room to change.

CHAPTER 22

On the ride back home, Steve, driving his own car with Donna, his only passenger, gave her the camera disc to give to Gary along with the name Edward Martin. Still puzzled about what it was all about, he figured he would let Donna give it to her brother and stay out of it.

"I can't tell you how scared Lynda seemed to be," he said out of the blue.

"Yeah, well, Lynda was always the strange one," she answered back. She took out her cell phone and dialed Lynda's home phone. "Let's see what she was doing so I can figure out what is going on with Gary."

Lynda's father answered the phone, to Donna's surprise. She updated him on what happened during the game and then asked what Lynda was doing taking pictures during the game. He told her that he didn't know everything yet, and he told her about the man who tried to take her camera. He then added that he was taking Lynda and her mother on a vacation out of town and was not sure when they would be back. He gave her his cell number and said that he wanted to talk to Gary as soon as possible. She could hear the distress in his voice and told him that she would have Gary call him tomorrow.

As they arrived home, the rest of the family was there already. Steve dropped Donna off and left. She went into the house and was told that Gary was in the shower, cooling off, and her mom had taken their aunt home.

"Did Gary take a change of clothes in with him or just a towel?" she asked Carol. Carol responded that she did see him go in with a change of clothes. "Good. I will be in his room, waiting to talk to him. Do *not* tell him I'm in there, waiting. I need to talk to him unprepared."

She went into his room and quietly looked around his desk. She saw the picture that he had in his helmet earlier. She shook her head and quietly thought, *Little bro, this is really fucking your brain up.* How did she not see this coming? She put the picture back down where she found it and sat down on his bed, waiting for him to come in.

"What are you doing in my room?" Gary said as he entered and saw her sitting there.

"We need to talk," she replied.

"No, we do not. Get out of my room."

"Not until I get some answers. What did Lynda have to take pictures of? What scared her? Do you know her father took her and her mother out of town tonight?" She barraged him with questions. She knew she had to get him to think about this all instead of bottling it up inside, which was what appeared to be happening. She knew her brother better than anyone, and she knew rebooting his brain was the only way to get through to him. He was quiet for a moment during the reboot and began to ponder her questions. Lynda was scared and now was in hiding?

"Where is Lynda now? I have to talk to her."

"You will have to wait until tomorrow. I talked to her father, and he gave me his cell number, but he wants to talk to you first."

This was no help. He needed to know what she found out that scared her so much. "I don't know who scared her."

"Well, her father told me that some guy tried to take her camera. She found two cops who questioned him. He was some security guy whose client was there, watching the game, and he suspected that she took pictures of his client. She found Steve and gave him this," she said as she gave him the camera disc. "Oh, and she mentioned the name Edward Martin, whoever the hell he is."

Gary's demeanor changed immediately. His mind was going a mile a minute, taking in all this new information. Donna noticed the change as he looked up at her and smiled. He then went over and gave her a big hug and proceeded to push her out of his room. "I have work to do. Give me Lynda's father's phone number. I will call him tomorrow."

As she passed Carol watching TV in the living room, she commented, "Your brother is weird."

Carol responded, "He's your brother too, and you knew him longer."

When Gary started thinking, he became hungry. As he did not eat much prior to the game, he came out of his room and made it to the kitchen to make himself a sandwich. As he sat there and ate his sandwich, his mom arrived home and was directed to the kitchen by Carol.

"Hi, Mom. I'm sorry I scared you earlier. I am feeling better now."

She looked at her son, and it was strange that he was now back to being the son she remembered, not that possessed soul she saw earlier that evening. "You want to tell me what happened to you today? Are you still angry about Carlos's death?"

"Well, yes and no. Being back in Miami brought back memories of Carlos and Manny and the Herta family, so yes, I was mad, but I know now I should not have used it out on the field. Is that boy I hurt going to be okay?"

"We'll know more tomorrow. He is in the hospital. They were going to have to set his collarbone and put him in a body cast. That's all I know right now."

"Can I go see him tomorrow? I really need to apologize to him."

"We will see. You have an appointment at the school with Father Tim. He wants you to go through grief consoling and is making himself available to do that. And you have to have a talk with Coach Lewis also. He is very worried about you."

This was going to take away his plans for the weekend. He now had a name to go with one of the faces. He had to continue to go through yearbooks from schools around Vermont from four to five years ago to discover Kim's real name. His first goal now was to talk to Coach Lewis and convince him that his actions were something other than anger about Carlos's death. If it got out that he knew Carlos, that would prompt the kidnappers to no longer look at him as a target. He had to maintain separation from the other kidnappings, or they would get away with killing Carlos. It was stupid of him to lose control like he did. He remembered what Father Tim had told him earlier: "Look into the heavens." He had to find his way back, and he had to do it now.

He looked at the clock and noticed it was close to eleven thirty. He had to get some sleep as he had a busy day tomorrow.

He knocked on Donna's door, as he could tell she was still awake. He handed her back the disc and asked her to hide it for now and he would get it from her on Sunday. She complied, still not knowing what this was all about, but was pleased that her brother trusted her with it for safekeeping. He went back to his room and crawled into bed thinking about his father.

Dad, stay with me. I am going to need you, was his final thoughts before drifting into a deep sleep.

CHAPTER 23

As the four of the team got into the car, Jerry turned to Eddie and said, "Our target may be small, but he's a little ass kicker. You sure you going to be able to handle him?"

"Come on, boss. He's a kid. I'd squash him like a bug and feed him to the gators."

"What happened to your hand? You are bleeding," Lauren called out in concern.

"Just some little bitch with a camera taking pictures. I thought she got you two in a shot and tried to grab her camera, and she scratched me with these dagger fingernails. Don't worry. I caught up with her with two cops and got them to let me look at the photo files. All clear. She must have been part of the school newspaper, just taking crowd shots. She moved over to the other stands."

"What was your cover story?" Jerry asked.

"I showed them my security ID. Told them I was protecting my client, who was there with his daughter to watch his nephew play in secret. They didn't take down any information, so no report was going to be filed."

"Hey, his daughter? You think I would pass for his daughter?" Lauren interjected.

Eddie was smiling. "They never asked me to point you two out, but yes…you could pass for his daughter." Jerry and Miguel started to laugh, which just pissed her off even more.

She responded with, "Well, it must be because you look like an old fart, Jerry, or do you want me to start calling you Dad?"

When the laughter was finished, Jerry said, "Okay, enough of the jokes now. We take the rest of the weekend off. Meeting at the office at 0900 Monday. This all goes down in two weeks, so let's finish up the loose ends."

CHAPTER 24

Gary was awake early that morning, especially for a Saturday. He decided to stay away from the chat rooms and blocked his presence online. He immediately went back to the yearbook website and continued looking for Kim's soccer team photo. He could tell that she had scanned it from a yearbook, because he noticed at the base of the photo, it looked like there was writing underneath that was cut off, perhaps noting the team player's name. Only the partial tops of the letters showed, so she did not move the picture high enough on the scanner. By the fourth yearbook that morning, he had found her. She was a younger version of the woman he saw at church and the picture of the woman he took at Haulover Pier. Lauren Butchart was her name. He had two names now out of the four suspects.

He did a search of the two names, Lauren Butchart and Edward Martin, to see if they were ever related in any news article, but did not get any hits. He did a background check on both and got the general information on both of them. Both had no current addresses in the last three years. He had to wait for the criminal background checks, so he decided to take a break and get some breakfast.

His mom was in the kitchen along with everyone else this morning except Steve, but he soon found out that he was on the way. He was reminded by his mom not to get too involved as he had to be at the school to talk to Father Tim and Coach Lewis.

"Hey, why are going to school on a Saturday? You made a big hit, and that guy got hurt. Isn't that what happens when you play football? I don't even see why you were removed from the game," Donna said in defense of her brother.

"It's okay. No big deal. They just want to talk to me about my attitude and coping with Carlos's death," Gary responded, as he did not want his sisters to get involved. "I'll jump in the shower after I eat, Mom, and get ready." He paused. "Hey, I forgot to ask, Who won last night?"

"You did. You didn't get to watch the second half, when the Wildcats got slaughtered, 63–24," Carol popped in as they all went to the kitchen for breakfast. "Coach Lewis must be really pissed at you today."

"Something tells me that he won't be that pissed off at me." Gary looked at his mother with a concerned look.

"But he—"

Carol was cut off by their mother. "What Gary is referring to is that…well, I should be the one to tell you girls this. I have been seeing the coach for the last three months."

The girls were stunned that they were not told. "Three months? You tell Gary and not me?" Donna retorted.

"Or me?" Carol added to be included in the conversation.

Their mother cut them off again. "I didn't tell Gary anything. His brain figured it out all by himself. It doesn't matter, anyway. Charles will take care of the situation, but Gary has to go through grief consoling with Father Tim."

Carol was a bit confused, but Donna was starting to understand what was going on with her brother. Not about his secrecy with Lynda and the photo disc, but that did give explanation about his distant attitude and anger. It must be hard on Gary to have all this brain power and not be able to use it with a friend having died like he did. She thought, *Gary must really feel useless right now.* If she only knew how far from the truth her summations were.

"I think I have a better idea. I'm taking Gary to the beach tomorrow to surf," Donna added, and Mom agreed. Gary started to smile as he also thought it was a great idea.

They finished breakfast, and Gary went to his room to get a change of clothes. Before he went into the bathroom, he knocked on Donna's door. She came to the door, and he asked her when they were going tomorrow so he could call Pattie to invite her.

"No, no. When I said you were going to go surfing, I meant it was going to be just you and Dad. No Patti or Steve or any of your other friends. It will just be you, me, and Dad. I'm staying on the beach. I am giving up my Sunday for you, so be ready at 9:00 a.m. Oh, here is Lynda's dad's phone number. Make sure you call him today."

He asked if he could use her cell phone to make the call.

"Yeah, but stay out of my messages, or you will not like where I put it if you do."

Gary nodded, agreeing with her terms.

He called Lynda's dad and caught a lot of cursing and attitude from him from the beginning. He refrained from telling him the real reason he asked her to take the pictures. He didn't trust him to stay out of what he was doing by going to his mother or, even worse, the police. He did ask him to call his old colleagues at the *Miami Herald* to leave Carlos's death out of the article where he broke that guy's collarbone as a result of him being distraught about his friend's death. He added, "Out of respect for the Herta family to keep Carlos's name out of the article." He said he would make the call. He did not tell Gary where he took his family, and Gary really didn't want to know. He apologized to him again about the attack on Lynda. He didn't know who that guy was and why he attacked her. Gary was an effective liar. He hung up the phone and continued to get ready for his meeting with Father Tim.

CHAPTER 25

As Gary and his mother arrived at the school, they went directly to the office to find out where Father Tim was. It being Saturday, there was very little activity at the school. They were directed to the chapel, where Father Tim had set up to have his talk with Gary. On the way, they ran into Sister Jean, who invited Marie to the teachers' break room for coffee while her son was with Father Tim. Sister Jean had apparently been made aware of the altercation during the game the previous night. She tried hard not to smile at Gary upon seeing him as to allude that this all was serious; however, she loved her favorite student and gave out a smile regardless.

"Gary, you would think you are smart enough to avoid the devil, but you keep inviting him to your games of wit."

Gary looked at her and thought that if she had any idea what was going on with him and why, she would concur that was indeed what was happening. He was definitely going against the devil for justice for Carlos, and to him, the devil was afraid.

"Don't worry, Sister, the devil has nothing on me."

She put her hand on Gary's head and said a silent prayer, and at the end, she said out loud, "Amen." Both Gary and his mother said, "Amen," in response.

"You know where the chapel is. Go, Father Tim is waiting for you. Take your time. We will be in the break room when you are finished."

Upon entering the chapel, he saw Father Tim sitting in the front pew. He was expecting Father to ask him if he wanted him to hear Gary's confession. But Father Tim had other ideas.

"So, Gary, let's just talk. You have been at SCC for several months now. How do you like it here?"

Gary was confused with that question and thought immediately that sounded like he was going to get expelled for his attitude.

"I like it a lot. Am I going to be expelled for hurting that guy last night?" He figured it would be better to find out early and hope that his intuition was wrong.

"No. We like you here also. I have read all your teachers' evaluations, and you bring a new challenge to their classes. Some think you not only came here to learn but to teach also. You appear to be thinking all the time and come up with very interesting questions. It makes the other students use your questions to learn from the answers. In other words, you help your teachers bring out the best of the other students. That's a very positive asset for us at SCC. But then we have this attitude lately that counter this. Your mother and Coach Lewis are concerned that something is going on with you to affect your attitude this way. That is what we are here to talk about. Anything you want to say about that?"

"I wasn't aware until last night that my attitude had changed. I don't know, but I just got angry last night. Thinking back more, I have had other instances. Right now, I am angrier with myself that I put that guy in the hospital. I guess I just lost control."

Father Tim was not convinced. He had gotten to know Gary well and took it as being played.

"I think it's a lot more than that. You are not being honest with me, or yourself, for that matter. Please tell me what is making you angry."

Gary's attempts at fooling Father Tim did not work. He wanted to keep the conversation as his problem without involving Carlos's death and his attempt to catch the kidnappers who had killed him. He decided to give him a partial truth.

"I've grown to like this school, but at first this would not have been my choice. My parents put me on the list years ago, and being accepted changed my life a lot. I had to adjust to coming here, from competing for a position on the football team and then not being allowed by Mr. Browning, getting beaten up on my first day of school, and then having a longtime friend die during a kidnapping. I am not afraid of challenges, but I think I have had my share of them since moving here. I guess I just need a break." Gary let out a small sigh, like he just got a weight off his shoulders. He hoped that worked at swaying Father Tim from probing more.

"I can understand all that, but anger is not the way to react to coping with this. You are not alone in anything, Gary. You competed and won your position with the team. You and your mom went down and, as I was told, overcame Mr. Browning's attempt to stop you from playing. I also was told by Sister Jean that some of the football team jumped in and stopped you from taking any further beatings that first day. You have a lot of support here. Your teachers, coaches, and classmates are all behind you. Your family loves you, and most importantly, your father is watching you. Use your poem and keep looking into the heavens. Your father is listening, and don't forget, God the Father is also. Keep him in your heart and there will be nothing to be afraid of or angry with. Your friend Carlos is sitting with God right now. Put away your anger."

"I will, Father. My sister is taking me alone to the beach tomorrow to go surfing with my dad. She already gave me the same advice. I'd invite you, but she already warned me that I have to talk to Dad alone, and if anyone just showed up, she would drown them and send them back with Dad to heaven. You think I was angry? You have not met my sister."

"Maybe someday I will. She seems to be on the same team as I am. So what are your plans today?"

"My mom is taking me to the hospital to see how that guy I put in there is doing, and to apologize for unloading on him as I did."

"What is the young man's name? I would like to go down there tomorrow to wish a quick recovery."

"His name is Brad Roberts. I hope he heals well. I understand he already committed to Auburn next year, and I hope he doesn't lose his scholarship because of this."

"I will be praying for him and for you also. Have you thought where you would like to go to college?"

"It's either University of Miami or Georgia Tech. I want to go into engineering."

"Both are good choices. Okay, last thing, I am available to hear your confession now, if you would like."

"Sure, Father. Bless me, Father, for I have sinned. My last confession was…"

CHAPTER 26

Gary was up early the next morning and jumped in the shower before anyone else was awake. He made it an issue to be ready to go to church this morning to see Patti. He knew he could not invite her to the beach but wanted to use the opportunity to see her outside of school before Monday.

He arrived, and Patti was waiting outside for him. Her family had already gone in and found seats. They made their way to the seats that were saved for them while waving at other classmate that also went to the same church. He noticed that Kim, or should he say Lauren, now that he knew her true identity, sitting in the last row. This was a good sign. This meant that they were still interested in him as a target. With two weeks before he was supposed to meet Kim, it was conclusive that he had to be the only one they were looking at. He paid no more attention to her as he sat down and followed the Mass as it began.

After Mass concluded, Gary had enough time to take Patti on a walk to be alone to talk. He did not take her hand, although he wanted to. He remembered that he had told Lauren that he and Patti broke up, and had to keep that appearance in play in the event they were still being watched.

"Gary, are you okay?" Patti asked with a concerned look on her face.

"I'm good. I just lost myself Friday night."

"Yeah, I have never seen you so angry like you were. Why so angry?"

He did not like lying to her, so he decided to try a little bit of honesty. "It's just that, I think it was just because I was in South Miami and I saw all the Herta family in the stands, all except Carlos.

He wasn't there because he is dead. I got angry and took it out on that running back." He paused as a tear formed in his right eye. "I didn't mean to hurt him." He was not acting. Patti tried to hug him to comfort him, but he held her back from doing do. Still focused on his mission, he had to maintain his distance from her and hope he could make it up to her later when this was all behind them.

Patti now was hurt by his rejection and backed away. "Call me when you get all your shit together, then. In the meanwhile, don't talk to me until you do." She walked away angry to find her parents. Gary followed behind slowly, thinking, *Well, that didn't go well.*

As Gary got back to the church, Donna was there and did not look happy. He looked at his watch and noticed the time was a little past ten o'clock. "I told you we would leave for the beach at nine, not ten!" she said in an agitated voice. "It's a good thing Dad would wait for you, or I'd cancel the whole day I was giving up for you."

Gary gave her a quick grin and replied, "I love you, Donna!"

"Shut up and get your ass in the car. Your wet suit is in the back seat. You can change on the way."

He jumped in the back seat to comply with his sister's orders.

Later, Gary jumped out of the back seat and proceeded to unlatch the surfboard from the roof racks on the car. Donna opened the trunk to get the beach chair and towels and started to walk over to the ocean.

"Hey!" Gary shouted out to his sister. "You aren't going to help me get my board off the car?"

She looked back briefly and said, "I put the damn thing up there myself. I'm sure a strong football player like yourself can handle it."

He shook his head and proceeded to remove the board himself.

As he approached the shoreline, he stopped to look at the waves, the wind, and the sun. It was a rough day to surf. "Dad, I hope you waited for me to get here, because these waves look like they are going to kick my ass." He proceeded to enter the water and quickly jumped on his board and paddled out to find a wave.

As he got out to pick his first wave, he stopped and sat up on his board and rode the rough waters, taking in the up-and-down movement of the sea around him. He had other surfers near him, to whom he gave a sign to go ahead of him. He wanted to think a bit before starting his run. Even though the waters were rough, it had a calming effect on him. He thought about his progress on catching the kidnappers. There was still a lot to learn about them. He had tracked down Lauren's identity but still had to get the other three. He had to review the pictures Lynda had taken, to see if there was any clue to the tech guy. Also, they must have a place picked to secure him after they took him. All the time he was thinking, he thought of his dad, on how much he would disapprove of what he was doing. He would be the only one who would understand why he was doing it. His mind turned to Patti, as he had really upset her this morning. He didn't want to involve her in any of his plans. If the plan went south, he could be putting her and others in trouble. He thought of his family and looked up to see Donna waving at him. He looked around and saw that there were no surfers in the water. Looking behind, he figured out why. There were serious storm clouds coming in. He saw the next wave and went for it. It was a big one, close to ten to twelve feet. As the wave rose up behind him and the board picked up speed, Gary decided he was not going to play it safe and started to stand up on the board and ride the wave in. Football had strengthened his legs, and it showed as he maintained his balance and moved his board in front of the wave to get maximum speed and control. As he got to the shallow waters close to the shores, he jumped off his board and walked his board to the beach. Donna was running into the water to help him out.

"What the fuck were you doing out there? Daydreaming?" she screamed at him. "You could have been killed!"

Gary plopped to the ground, completely out of breath.

"You can't rest now. We have to get your board tied down and back home."

Gary drudged his body up with the help of his sister as two other surfers ran up and grabbed the board and carried it to the car. As Gary and Donna dried off, the surfers put the board on the roof and tied it down. One of the surfers started to say, "Dude, that was one hell of—"

Donna stopped him with a finger pointed at him and said one word. "Don't." They backed away without saying another word.

Gary had to hold back his laughter and went with a small smile which he hid from his sister. When Donna was pissed, even strangers knew to walk away.

On the drive back home, the weather got worse. Gary, sitting in the passenger seat, closed his eyes to continue his thinking. He did not get a full chance to channel his father but got the feeling that the weather had much to tell him, that someone wasn't liking his thinking. It didn't really matter if his father approved of his actions; regardless, he knew his father would be there to catch him if he needed it.

As soon as they reached the top of the driveway, Donna turned off the car and Gary heard the locks click. Donna, now calmed down a bit during the drive back home, turned to her brother, holding back whatever anger she had for him. "Okay, that's it! What the fuck is going on with you? I want to know right now."

"There is nothing wrong with me," Gary answered.

"Oh, we are going there now? You think I can't see through your bullshit? Gary, this is Donna here. I know you. You have been keeping to yourself, your head in your computer all the time. Everyone knows something's going on inside that brain of yours, and you won't talk to anyone about it. At first, I thought this was one of your schemes you were up to, but they are usually just a couple of days, not months." Her voice eased a bit as her eyes started to tear up. "I'm scared, Gary, and I don't know why. Please tell me what's going on."

Gary looked at his sister and saw how distraught she was. She had been a rock since their father died, and he hated to see her this way. However, he knew if he told her, she would tell their mother, and everything would stop. That would not be right, not for him. He was two weeks away from completing this. "There is nothing going on. You have to trust me."

"Give me a reason. You want my trust, yet you still won't tell me anything."

"I can't tell you anything. There is nothing to tell," Gary responded. He just lied to his sister again. It was an outright lie, something he never did to Donna. What was worse was that he did it knowing that Donna knew he was lying. But it didn't matter at this point. He was going to complete his mission, and he would not be stopped. He was alone in this. After what happened to Lynda, he was not going to involve any of his family or friends. He needed to keep them out of it and safe.

"When you stop lying to me and yourself, please tell me what is happening with you. I will be here to listen when you are ready to talk," Donna said, wiping away the tears from her eyes. "Get the board off the car and get it in the garage before the rain catches up here." She hit the garage door opener and left him to put away his board alone.

Gary complied, quickly untying and removing the board and moving it into the garage. As he started to close the garage door, a car pulled into the driveway. It was Coach Lewis. It was odd that his mom would invite him to the house; however, he surmised that he was invited for Sunday dinner. He stopped the door from closing and quickly hit the button to reopen the door as the rain started coming down. He wanted to give Coach Lewis a shorter run into the house.

"Hey, Coach. Are you here for dinner?"

"That's the plan, Gary. Your mom is a good cook, and she said she is making your favorite, chicken Parmesan?"

"Yeah, it is, and it is the best."

"Good. Keep eating it. You can use about another ten to fifteen pounds by next year's football season."

The two went into the house. As his coach went to say hello to the rest of the family, he ran to the bathroom to jump into the shower to wash off the sand from his body before dinner. As he stood under the water, he thought about the coach mentioning next year's football season. He had given it some thought, that with what he did in the last game, he wouldn't be allowed to play. He put it out of his mind for now, as there were more important things he was concerned with. He dried off and got dressed for Sunday dinner.

CHAPTER 27

During the ride to school on this particular morning, Gary was deep in thought about the days to come. In one case, it was a relief that football season was over for this year. It usually was depressing that the practices were over and the readiness for and playing the weekly games were done for until next year. However, at this time, he had other things to concern himself with. He anticipated that the background checks on Lauren and Edward Martin should be in his inbox very soon. He wasn't sure if he had much of a change of getting anything on the latter, as Martin was a common name and he had to guess at his approximate age for the profile. He also knew that he would run into Patti today, and he was not sure how he was going to handle it. He hated to treat her like he did; however, he was thinking more over about the danger he put Lynda in, and he did not want to put Patti or any other friends and family members in the same risk. These were people who had their last victim die on them, and they turned around and started to set up their next target without lying low, which was not a logical move on their part. That made them way ahead of him on their plans. He had two weeks to figure who they were and what their overall plan was.

As Gary walked through the hallways to get to his homeroom, he greeted may students with small talk on the way. No one mentioned anything about the game on Friday night, of which he was relieved. It wasn't until he ran into Mike that the topic came up.

"So did you go see that guy you flattened at the game last Friday?" Mike threw out at him immediately. Gary was a bit hit off guard with the question, but seeing it was Mike, he gave him a pass.

"Yeah, I did. He's okay. They had him in an upper-body cast after they put his shoulder back together. The doctor said it was a clean break and it went back together easy enough and they installed some clamp with pins to keep it together while it heals. They told him six months, so he should be able to play next year."

"Good. What about you? Are you getting in any trouble for the hit?"

"I had a meeting with Father Tim on Saturday morning that I don't want to talk about."

"Nay, that's okay. That would be too much information, anyway. As long as you aren't going to get suspended or anything."

"No, that's not going to happen."

The two quickly got to their homerooms prior to the first bell.

The rest of the morning went without incident, until lunchtime, when Gary ran into Patti. She looked a little upset and hurting when she looked at him. She did not sit at the same table with him. When he finished his lunch, he went over and quietly asked her if she would meet him in the parking lot after school. She agreed and put out a small smile. He was not prepared for the smile, so he did not know if it was a forced smile or a sign that she had forgiven him for the way he had treated her. He would ponder that for the rest of the afternoon.

As the last class was finished, he started to make his way to the parking lot for his talk with Patti. He was stopped by Father Tim, who cut him off to see how he was doing. He figured if he tried to push him off, he would think Gary was still dealing with problems in his own head, so he took about a five-minute delay to talk to him so that he would think Gary was moving past his problems. He ended the conversation by mentioning that he had to get to the parking lot to talk to Patti. A boy wanting to talk to a girl would give Father Tim the idea that Gary's mind was going in the right direction. Father Tim gave him a smile and sent him on his way. Gary believed that his submission worked. He made it the parking lot in time before Patti got in her mom's car. Patti said something to her mother through the open window and met Gary halfway as he approached her.

"Sorry I'm late. Father Tim stopped me in the hallway to ask how I was doing," Gary said as they met.

"Good question. So how are you doing?" Patti answered quickly.

"I'm doing okay. That's what I wanted to tell you. And to apologize for the way I acted yesterday."

"And so apologize!"

Gary's emotions took over at that point as he looked into her eyes. He moved closer to her and said, "I'm sorry," and kissed her on the lips in front of everyone, including her mother. As Mom was now blowing the horn to get her daughter's attention, Gary said quickly, "I will call you tonight. I am in the middle of a project right now, and I will tell you all about it when it's complete. Two weeks and it should be over. Go, before your mom kills me."

"She won't. My sister might. Call me tomorrow night. Something tells me I won't be able to accept phone calls tonight." Tempting fate, she leaned over and kissed Gary goodbye and turned to go back to the car.

CHAPTER 28

Gary got home and went straight to his room and booted up his computer. He quickly changed out of his school clothes and opted for shorts and a T-shirt for comfort. He went straight to his email and saw that the background checks had arrived. He opened up the one with Lauren's name and started to review the information. He sent the file to his printer to be printed out so he could make notes on it. She was born in Braydon, Vermont, and was twenty-two years old. She graduated from Braydon High School, which confirmed her identity in the yearbook picture that she sent him. He moved on to her current and prior addresses and noted that she primarily lived in Braydon except for a brief time she lived in Boston. She lived at two different addresses in Boston. He looked up the first address, which indicated to be an apartment complex. The other was a house address. That seemed odd to him, as she was noted to be single and never married. Her employment records noted she worked as a waitress during that time. He went back online to do a search on the ownership of the house in Boston, and the results showed that it was owned by a man named Gerald Hall. He wrote the name down to follow up later. He then moved on to her arrest report, and she did have a run-in with the law after high school. It indicated she was arrested three times, once for shoplifting and twice for solicitation.

"So she was a prostitute?" Gary pondered.

He looked further on her arrest record and noticed that the arresting officer on the solicitation charges were both a Detective Jerry Hall. Jerry Hall? Could that be Gerald Hall, whose house she was living in? Gary became excited with this new information. He was starting to connect the dots and was driven at finding out more of this team who had killed Carlos.

He was not ready for the distraction of someone knocking on his door.

"What do you want? I am busy. Leave me alone!" Gary screamed loudly toward the door.

"Dinner's ready. Why are you yelling?" Carol's voice came back to answer his tirade.

"All right. I'll be right there," Gary retorted. He didn't want to scream at his little sister and surely did not want to upset his mother by having dinner wait on him. He had caused her enough worry in the past months. He put away his notes and went to dinner. He would put on a good front and then come back after dinner to continue his research.

After dinner was complete, he returned to his room to continue going through the information he had gotten. There was not much more he showed on Lauren Butchart. As he reviewed the information that he had gotten on her, he started to have some mixed feelings on his past relationship with this woman. This was a girl he had considered his friend, and now he was finding out she was part of the crew that killed Carlos. He had to change that. He had decided to dehumanize her. He was no longer going to call her Lauren or Kim. From now on, her designation was Bait. He pulled out his notepad and wrote on the top of the first four pages the new designations, Bait, Boss, Tech, and Muscle. That was what he would now relate them as. He wrote all the information he had about Lauren on the Bait page.

He then moved on to Edward Martin, who he felt was Muscle. He had chosen three Edward Martins for the background checks. All three did not include much information, and unfortunately no pictures that he could match with the picture taken at the marina or from Lynda's photos taken at the football game. There was a notation from Martin No. 3 that he was an ex-Marine. As the Edward Martin he was looking for was a man of a strong healthy stature, he highlighted No. 3 as his best possible candidate. He noted any information from each three regardless and hoped it might cross-reference with information from background check for Boss, who he surmised as being Gerald Hall. He did a search on Gerald Hall with a sub-search noting "police" and "Boston." He immediately got a full bio on Detective Jerry Hall. He had worked as part of the vice department, which put him in a position that would include Lauren as part of his arrests. Also, he was part of the federal task force on missing children. The head of the task force was Special Agent James Kelly, FBI. This was disturbing news, as he had always thought that Agent Kelly was very reparable and concerned about the children that were being kidnapped for ransom. He noted it on his information sheet with a question mark and a notation in parathesis: "(coincidence)." He went over his conversation with Agent Kelly and put another notation as kidnappers seemed to be ahead of every move that the FBI was involved. Perhaps this was why they had been so successful, because the Boss knew how the FBI operated. Also, because he was part of the task force, his closeness to Agent Kelly was why he had been overlooked as a possible suspect. The Boss was previously Captain Hall, USMC. Special Forces. He just connected the Muscle No. 3 with the Boss with a possible military connection. He had to do more research to confirm it.

Gary had to connect faces with each one. He had his pictures from the football game and Haulover, but he had to be able to confirm the names. He surmised that the FBI was not coming up with any leads because they didn't know what he knew. He picked up the connection between Kim/Lisa and Carlos. He put together the connection of a woman he took a picture of in Miami-Dade County and a woman who showed up at his church in Palm Beach County. Most importantly, he knew that he was the next target of the kidnappers. The kidnappers had clearly overestimated him. Gary was way aware that he was putting himself in extreme danger; however, he had to bring Carlos's killers to justice. He decided to try Facebook to find additional information on the kidnaping team. Time was becoming short. He noticed the time was getting late and realized his mom would be in shortly to tell him to shut it down and go to bed. This was a good time to stop for the night, although he knew that he wasn't going to just stop thinking about it. However, just as the kidnappers had been steps ahead of the FBI, he had to keep similarly ahead of his mother. He would go to bed and sit in the darkness and put to work the best computer he had, his own mind.

He stripped off his shorts and climbed into bed with just his underwear and T-shirt on. Once comfortable, he said a quick prayer to his father, asking him to keep him strong and safe on the plans he was going to put himself in. He believed his father was looking down on him and would approve of his actions.

As he lay back on his pillow, he stared upward in his dark room and began to run through everything he had found so far. He thought of all the times he had talked to Kim, a.k.a. Lauren, online and really felt hatred for this person. Although she was probably the most innocent of the four, she was still the first contact with all the victims. If she weren't that good, this team of kidnappers would not work. The Boss was very smart and calculating, the true professional of the group. He would like to practice his kicking on him the most. The Muscle probably had the most contact with the victims and didn't do his job as well as he should have, or Carlos would still be alive. The Tech was probably the most critical of the group due because they hadn't been caught yet. To set up the internet connections and make them disappear so they could not be traced back to their operation was pure genius. Gary couldn't do that, so he felt he wouldn't begin to know how to trace it back to them now even though the IP addresses were still active and in use and the FBI was not aware that they were running an ongoing operation. He needed to find a computer geek who knew how that could be done. He recapped everything again and stored it in his internal memory. He had some big days ahead of himself the next week.

Eventually, he wore his mind down to the point that he drifted to sleep. Tomorrow was another day.

CHAPTER 29

Gary arrived at school early the next day to begin his search for some-one who knew enough about computers to help him find the Tech. He knew that Mr. Hill, his homeroom teacher, aside from teaching English, also was teaching computer science as an advanced class for seniors only. He had to get in early to pick Mr. Hall's brain about IP addresses. He was in luck, as Mr. Hall was in early this morn-ing. He had to approach him carefully, though, as Gary's reputation as a genius was well-known by all his teachers. He decided regard-less that his best way in this case was to act ignorant of computers. He brought a printed copy of an email sent to him by Manny. He had come up with a series of questions to show his ineptness about computers so that Mr. Hall would feel delighted to help an assumed genius in a subject that was not one of his strengths.

"Mr. Hall, you know a lot about computers. Can you help me with understanding something?" Gary said to open the conversation.

"Sure, Gary. What do you need to know?" Mr. Thompson replied with a big smile. He knew that if Gary asked a question, he must really be stumped, and he was eager to help.

Handing him Manny's email, he asked if the series of numbers printed on the top of the email was the IP address of the sender or his own. Mr. Thompson went on to explain that it was the IP address of the sender and proceeded to give Gary a lesson on IP addresses and what they were used for.

Gary continued with his next question. "So is it possible to trace an IP address to find the location of the sender?"

"Yes and no. You can't get an exact location of the address. It will give a general location of the sender."

"Okay, so how do you get the general location of the sender?"

"Why do you want to know how to do that?"

"My friend Manny is going on a vacation on Saturday and won't be back until January. His family is going to Texas and on to Arizona. Manny's cousin was the boy who was kidnapped and sent back dead. I want to be able to track where he goes. I know I could just ask him where he is at, but this way will be more fun." He looked at Mr. Thompson and saw that he had bought his lie.

"All right, on your Windows operating system, open the Command prompt…"

He went on to explain how to trace the address, and Gary wrote down every step. He had told Kim last night that the area he lived was getting an upgrade in the cables on his internet provider service, so he would be off the internet for about a week. Knowing that not being able to communicate would complicate the mission, they would have to send an email to set the meeting up. He provided his email address so they could do just that. Gary was in control right now, and he felt empowered at that prospect. They had to set up the meeting so they could plan the kidnapping properly. He was in a good place to help them and himself. By setting the location early enough, he would be able to come up with a game plan to be a couple of steps ahead of them for a change. He had to also determine where their operation was set up, so he could give the FBI a heads-up so they could move in before the Tech could delete their existence and lose valuable information for prosecution. Gary's mind was going in several directions in every moment. At one moment he was enjoying the ride he had his brain going, but in the end, his main motivation always brought him back to reality: bringing Carlos's murderers to justice.

When he arrived home, he went straight to his room and turned on his computer. As he had anticipated, the Bait's email was in his inbox with the location of their meeting. They were to meet behind the Sawgrass Mill's Mall near the theater in Sunrise, Florida, next Saturday at 9:00 a.m. He knew the mall well, as they had driven up there several times in the past from Miami. He could get there on his own by getting on the Tri Rail train to Fort Lauderdale and switching to a bus that would take him to the mall. Gary surmised that this was also a clue to where they would be bringing him after he was kidnapped. That location had to be close or accessible to that location. The only remote area where it would be hard to trace were the Everglades themselves. Time was running out.

He followed Mr. Hill's directions and traced the IP address to a location in Downtown Fort Lauderdale. He had already figured that they might have set up in a small office complex or warehousing area, where they could hack into several IP addresses to mask their true location. Downtown Fort Lauderdale would be like looking for a needle in a haystack. He had to go down there to physically scope out the area. This would be a good opportunity to practice his travel plans for next Saturday. He could not wait for the weekend to do this. Although it was not in his nature to do so, he had to skip school tomorrow to get this done. This would take some thinking on how to get this done without getting into trouble.

He had one more thing to look into before going to bed. He had to look into where in the Everglades could there be a place to hide him while they waited for the ransom. He typed into his search engine on residences or buildings in the Everglades. Other than the fishing camps, he came up with nothing. He thought for a bit and remembered that the Boss and the Muscle both served in the military. He changed his search to include military training facilities— abandoned. He got five hits on his search. All were accessible by airboat; however, only two had an existing structure still standing on it. The one closest to a fishing camp that rented airboats was noted to have existing power to the building. He had to check it out. He made a mental note to call Steve tomorrow to see if he wanted to take him fishing in the Everglades. They went once two years ago, and although Gary was not big into fishing then, he had to work on Steve to take him again anyway.

Early the next morning, Gary called Steve to set up a fishing trip this Saturday. Steve was all for it and confirmed with him he would pick him up at 7:00 a.m. on Saturday. He did ask Gary if he had cleared it with his mother, and of course, he lied and said she agreed. He would get her permission later, as he knew how to work his mom. He next called Mike and asked to tell his homeroom teacher that he would be late this morning and he would check in at the office when he got there. It was an honest excuse, as he did not expect to be all day in Fort Lauderdale. He had a quick breakfast and made some lame excuse for riding his bike to school for exercise this morning, and off he went.

The train station was three miles from his house. He did get the exercise he said he was going to have, as he made it in record time. He boarded the train with his bike and found a secluded seat away from everyone. He had about forty-five minutes to catch his breath and review his notes. He took out the pictures of the football game that Lynda took. He studied each face over and over to remind him of his four targets. He did not want to run into any of them. He remembered that he purposely wore a light sweatshirt with a hoodie. He raised the hoodie over his head and put on his sunglasses. A simple disguise that should keep his identity hidden. He continued to study his notes until the voice over the intercom stated that his stop was next. He quickly put all his notes together and put them back in his backpack, stood up, grabbed his bike, and made his way to the exit doors.

As soon as he was out of the train station, he jumped on his bike and made his way to the location his search provided. He looked around, and there were four possible buildings that his targets could be using. He eliminated two of the buildings as they were fifteen and eighteen stories high and were high-priced office rental spaces, and he did not think that his targets would pay that much for temporary use. The other two were smaller structures with retail spaces on the ground level. The building on the corner had a small coffee shop, so he locked up his bike in the bike racks in front and went into the coffee shop and sat and waited. He ordered a blueberry muffin and a Coke and just looked at the people as they passed by. It wasn't long before he noticed a familiar face enter the coffee shop. It was the Bait.

She came in and ordered three coffees, paid the woman behind the counter, and left. She never looked around the shop, and he watched her as she walked across the street and entered the building. She never looked back, so he was sure she did not notice him. He quickly got up, leaving his muffin and soda behind, and ran across the street to enter the building twenty seconds behind her. He saw her getting in the elevator and got there in time to see the elevator stop on the fifth floor. He kept looking and noticed that the elevator was on the way back down. He looked around and found the stairs and quickly opened the door and stepped inside. He looked out the door, still within sight of the elevator, and as the elevator doors opened, it was empty. She got off on the fifth floor. He decided it would be safe to walk the stairs up to that level, but first he needed to check the building directory. There were eight offices noted on the directory. He took out his notebook and quickly wrote down the names of the businesses that occupied those offices. He went back to the stairway and started his incline up to the fifth floor.

He slowly opened the stairway door and peeked into the hallway. He heard low talking out of sight from the doorway. He listened to the conversation as well as he could; however, he was not able to make out all the words they were saying. He did notice that one of the voices was a woman's. She talked faster than the man with an accent that he did not recognize. It was not a foreign accent, as the English she was speaking was fluent. Having lived in South Florida all his life, he did not encounter other American accents from around the country. He knew he was dealing with at least two of the kidnappers who were from Vermont and Boston, so perhaps it was one of those. He made a note to go online tonight and listen to different accents and see if what he was hearing matched.

He started to hear footsteps as the conversation ended. They did not go to the elevators as he assumed they went in the opposite direction. He confirmed that assumption as he heard the sound of the footsteps fade. He needed to look around the floor but was not sure that was a safe thing to do. He quickly came up with a plan and ran down the stairs to the ground floor. As he arrived on the street, he looked around and saw a grill restaurant a block away. He went in and ordered a hamburger and fries and requested they put it in a big delivery bag. He got back to the office building, went quickly through the front door, and shot straight to the elevators as if he belonged there.

He took the elevator to the fourth floor and went down the hallway where the bathroom doors were located. He knocked on the door, pushed it open partway, and said in a deep voice, "Maintenance. Anyone in here?" There was no answer, and so he proceeded to go in. He went to the back stall and locked the door. He took off his jacket and shirt and opened his backpack and took out a bra that he had borrowed from Donna's drawer. He slipped it on and put some socks he brought along to fill out each cup. He was thankful his sister was not as big up top as their mother was. He took out a pink blouse and slid it on over the bra and down past his belt. He saw how girls dressed, so tucking in the blouse was not going to be a good look. He pulled out a brunette wig and carefully placed it on his head, positioning the hair to finish out his look. He put his jacket on and pulled his hood over the wig carefully and did not zip it up. Upon putting back on his sunglasses, he walked out of the stall with his backpack and bag of food with him. He gave himself a quick look in the mirror, where he now looked like a teenage girl. He walked out of the bathroom and proceeded to the elevators. He traveled to the fifth floor and exited to the left, going in the side opposite the direction from where he had heard the conversation earlier. He went down the hallway and noticed that all the offices had door signs that were made for the specific business. He got to the end and went around to the other hallway past the elevators. He made his way past all the doors and noticed the same premade signs for each office, until he got to the last office, which had a printed sign. The name of the sign said, "Micro Products."

He took out his pen, wrote the office number, 505, on the bag in big letters, and knocked on the door.

The door opened, and there stood the Muscle. Gary, without missing a beat, said, "I have a delivery for Mike from Tony's up the street."

Eddie turned around for a second and said, "Miguel, did you order food from Tony's?"

Miguel answered, "Not me."

Eddie turned back to Gary and told him he got the wrong office. Gary apologized and turned and left. He heard the door close as he walked away. He had gotten a good view of the office and noticed all the computers and equipment in the room. He decided to take the stairs to the second floor and went in the women's bathroom to change back to being a boy again. He got into the stall and took a deep breath. He could not believe he pulled that off. He took the stairway to the ground floor and exited the building. He got back to his bike and made it back to the train station to get back to school. He had to wait ten minutes for the train to arrive but took that time to eat the food he bought.

He got back to school at ten thirty, locked up his bike, and went to the office to sell why he was late.

CHAPTER 30

Gary spent lunchtime in the library, where he would be able to write down everything he had learned that morning. He found an empty table in the back, took out his notebook, and started to add all the information to his files. He knew now the Tech's first name was Miguel. He had to check on the Boss's and the Muscle's known associates to find the last name. He figured, with an operation this tight, everyone in the group had known one another for a long time. It just made sense to him. He put his notebook back in his backpack. He closed his eyes to think for the rest of time before running to his next class.

On the way, he ran into Patti. She asked where he was this morning and why he was late. Gary answered her quickly by saying he rode his bike to school and got a flat. He hated to lie to her like that and hated even more that he had been lying to her several times in the last weeks. He only hoped that when this was all over, she would forgive him when she heard the whole truth.

He had just sat down in his algebra 2 class when Father Tim came into the classroom and requested that Gary be excused as he needed to talk to him. "Take him, Father. He's all yours, but bring him back in one piece. There are some in the class that still need his tutoring in order to pass," Sister Jean responded. There were chuckles from some of the other students. Gary was sure it was from the ones he didn't tutor at lunch.

He was curious what Father Tim wanted him for. He followed behind him all the way to his office without saying a word. He sat down on the couch as directed, and Father Tim sat in his usual cushioned chair across from the couch.

"Gary, your mother called me this morning and asked if I would talk to you about what's going on. She told me that you have been very distant from everyone. You seem to be keeping yourself detached from your sisters and your friends. She tells me you come home from school, eat dinner, and then lock yourself in your room for the rest of the evening. So tell me, what's going on?"

Gary was taken for a loop with that question. He had been so immersed with his plan on revenge for Carlos's death that he did not realize just how much his planning was affecting others. He did some quick thinking, knowing that Father Tim was not someone he could fool easily, so he decided to start by going with half-truths.

"I don't know. I have been feeling a bit stressed on what happened to my friend Carlos."

"That's not unusual, Gary. You are still going through some mourning after his death. I wish you had come to me earlier so we could talk about it more. The last time we talked after that enraged tackle which put that guy in the hospital, you did not mention anything about Carlos. Do you feel that you are responsible in some way because of his death?"

"No, I don't think so. I hadn't seen Carlos since I moved up to Riverside. I don't know if I could do anything even if I knew he was talking to someone online who wound up getting him killed. We didn't talk online, so I didn't know anyone he was talking to."

"If you did, do you think you would have known there was something wrong?"

"No. When Agent Kelly asked if I knew anyone he was talking to online, I could not give him an answer. Maybe if I did, I could have given him something that would help him find Carlos's killer."

"So you are feeling a bit of guilt over his death, or at least finding out who was responsible for it."

"Maybe. I think that they will eventually be caught." Gary threw that out there. He liked the guilt idea, so he decided to keep going in that direction. "I am just upset someone killed him and I can't help. I feel so useless."

"You are not useless. Just be a friend to Manny and the rest of the Herta family. Give them your love, prayers, and support. That's the best way to help everyone involved, especially yourself."

"I will. And thank you, Father, for the talk. I feel a little better now."

"Good. So what are your plans for the Christmas break? Doing anything special this year?"

"Not that I am aware of. This is the first Christmas in the new house. I think my mom and aunt Connie are going to cook up a storm and have everyone over for a big Italian dinner. Are you doing anything? You have my invite to come on over."

"I would love that. Ask your mom if she has room for an extra plate on the table, and get back to me."

"You got it. I better get back to my math class before it is over. Sister Jean likes to give us extra homework each weekend."

"Yes, you better get going. And, Gary, make sure you save a place for your father at that table. You know he will be there."

"Yeah, he will," Gary responded with a smile. The smile was important. He left Father Tim with the idea that he had helped Gary in some way with his little talk. Hopefully, he would report back to his mother that everything was okay and he could finish this little project without her worrying.

He got back to his math class just as Sister Jean was handing out a final homework assignment before midterm exams the next week. Math was one subject he was not concerned about passing midterms. He was going to disappoint some, however, as he would not have time to tutor his friends to prepare them for the tests. He has to put all his effort and time to finishing up his research on the kidnappers before the next weekend, when he himself got kidnapped. Only one more class for today and then he could go home and prepare for his fishing trip with Steve tomorrow. Big day and final week of putting his plan in action.

CHAPTER 31

Gary woke up early and quickly dressed for his day in the Everglades. He got out his portable GPS that once belonged to his father. They used it whenever they were fishing or camping, so they didn't get lost. However, today he would use it to locate the coordinates of the abandoned research center that he suspected was going to be his holding area when he got kidnapped. He put it in his backpack and went out to see if Steve had arrived. On his way to the kitchen, he ran into Steve walking through the door. He heard talking in the kitchen so assumed everyone was awake.

"Go get your rod and put it with mine. We will load up after we eat," Steve said with authority.

"Load up," Gary heard and responded quizzically, "Why did you take your gear out of the truck to reload it again?" He followed Steve into the kitchen.

"I'm not driving, he is," Steve said.

Sitting at the table, drinking his coffee, was Couch Lewis. Putting down his cup, he gave Gary a smile and said, "When your mom told me of your fishing excursion today, I volunteered to go with you. I haven't gone fishing for years."

Gary thought this was not a good idea. He knew he could manipulate Steve in going the direction he wanted to go, but with Coach Lewis, it was a much different scenario. He was always taking direction for his coach, not the other way around. He had an hour plus to rethink his new situation and had that time to come up with a new plan. He turned and went to the garage to comply with Steve's direction and returned as his mother was putting food on the table.

He was quiet during breakfast as he was uncomfortable with the position he was now put in. After breakfast was done, they loaded the fishing gear into Coach Lewis's car and off they went. It took every bit of the hour to get from Palm Beach County to West Broward's edge, which was nothing but the Everglades from there on. They got to the fishing camp, where Coach Lewis rented an airboat for the day. He was impressed as his coach sped away from the dock with reckless abandon. It was a side of his coach that Gary had never imagined. He checked his GPS and got his bearings and then pointed in the direction he wanted to go. The coach veered in that direction without hesitation. He took a quick breath as he was anticipating some trepidation from Coach Lewis. They went through a break in the sawgrass and kept following the open pathway until they got to a clearing. He saw a pole that protruded above the sawgrass past the clearing. He assumed that was the abandoned research center that he was looking for.

Coach Lewis stopped the boat, turned off the engine, and climbed down from the seat.

"Okay, guys, this looks like a good place to drop some lines in," Coach said as he grabbed his pole.

Gary, although disappointed that he didn't get to his destination, decided to go along and fish for bit to keep appearances right. He had a lot of time to come up with a reason to go exploring. He decided he would stand and fish instead of sitting down like the others.

"So, Gary, how is everything going with you?" Coach said to start a conversation.

"I'm doing okay," he responded, having picked up why his coach came along today. This was his mom's idea, to see if he would open up to him. He had to keep the talk in a way to control the answers he wanted to give. "Hey, thanks for taking us out here. Where did you learn to drive an airboat like that?"

"In the Army. I can drive anything. We had to."

"What did you do in the Army?" Gary quipped so he could keep the conversation away from him.

"Army rangers. I did two tours in Afghanistan. We went in first to do recon."

"Did you see a lot of fighting?"

"We did our share. I don't recommend it. Although jumping out of airplanes or rappelling out of helicopters was fun."

"Wow, I never took you for the daredevil type. I wish I could do that someday."

"Like I said, I don't recommend it. Besides, you are too smart to do crazy, foolish things like that."

"I don't know, Coach. I did take on Jimmy and took him to the ground." Gary thought, if his coach only knew of the crazy, foolish things he was planning on doing, he would be surprised.

They fished for about two hours. Gary got a few bites, while Steve and Coach caught and released a couple each. Coach tried to help Gary with some hints on what he was doing wrong, but he really was not into fishing today.

As they were wrapping things up, it was time to make his move.

"Coach, what's that pole sticking up over there?"

"Not sure. Let's go check it out," Coach replied. Gary was surprised how easy that was.

As they made it around the openings in the sawgrass, they finally approached an island in the middle of the surrounding tall sawgrass. Gary was optimistic that this had to be the place, because the pathway made by previously crushed sawgrass was probably caused by Eddie. The island had a metal building erected on it and a power pole confirming the structure had or had had power, as noted on the information he had found on the internet. Before getting to the island, they heard a hissing sound coming from the right in the sawgrass. Coach quickly turned the boat around and headed back the way they came.

"What's wrong, Coach?" Gary said with disappointment.

"Gators. There's probably a nest there. We do not want to get anywhere near it."

Gary was disappointed, to say the least, as he did get a chance to see the building he believed he would be held at.

As they made their way back to the fishing camp to return the airboat, he was deep in thought. He kept going over all the aspects of what was going to happen and what he was missing. He still had to find the identity of the Tech. He knew his first name to be Miguel.

He also knew the others all had previous relationships with the Boss, so he figured to check into his past relationships when he got home. He was close to putting all the information in order so when they kidnapped him, he could give as much to the FBI to make their case and convict these guys. He kept thinking in his mind, *For Carlos.* He had to get it done.

He thanked Coach for taking him fishing and went straight to his room to go over the information he had on Mr. Gerald Hall. He went to arrest records to see if he had ever arrested a tech guy, but he found nothing. He was into vice arrests, but no arrests involving computer crimes, such as identity theft or child porn. He was finding nothing but dead ends. No Miguel.

Just then, his mother called him for dinner, so he put everything down and took a break to eat. He figured he would clear his mind for a bit and start up again after dinner.

When dinner was finished, he realized he had an odor about him, as he had not showered after his fishing outing with Steve and the coach. He figured he would take a nice, hot shower to clean up and relax a bit. He grabbed a change of clothes and ran into the empty bathroom. As he got under a nice stream of hot water, he felt himself calming after a busy day. As he soaked himself, his mind began to think of the case again. He remembered the day he stood at the door of the office when he had said the name Mike; however, Eddie immediately thought he was referring to Miguel. Then he remembered that Eddie and Miguel must have been the two sitting together at the game that night, and he had a picture of him that Lynda took that night.

He washed himself off and quickly jumped out of the shower, dried himself, and got dressed. He pulled out the photo and began studying it. He never saw Miquel that day, only heard his voice. The face looked familiar, but he could not place it right away. He went back to his file on Gerald Hall and pulled out a picture of his Special Forces unit, and there it was. Tech Sergeant Miguel Santos was part of Jerry's unit. He had now identified all members of the group. He had them all. He was ready to meet them on Saturday. Soon this would all be over and Carlos would have his justice.

CHAPTER 32

He was up early Saturday morning. He showered and dressed quickly and had started toward the door when he was intercepted by Donna. He was informed that his mother and Carol had left earlier to go Christmas shopping with Aunt Connie. He had put all his notes in order and called Agent Kelley, telling him that he had some information that he wanted to provide for Carlos's case, and asked to meet him at the house at ten o'clock this morning to go over them. He wasn't going to be there. He should be kidnapped by that time. He asked Donna to let him in when he got there, and was out the door. He got on his bike and made it in record time to catch the train to Fort Lauderdale. It took three buses to get to the mall, but he got there fifteen minutes early. The mall was packed with shoppers, with only two weeks before Christmas.

Gary was curious how he was going to be isolated from the crowd to be kidnapped without being seen. He was going through all the different scenarios in his head until he just figured they had it all planned out, so he would just have to let it happen.

Right then he saw Eddie following him. He had made it to the movie theater, where he was to meet Kim. Suddenly, he heard a series of loud bangs across from the theater. As everyone turned to check the commotion, he felt a sharp pinch in his neck, and then darkness.

Eddie and Jerry had grabbed the boy's arms and moved him out the side door, where Lauren was waiting for them with a van. They shoved the boy into the van and drove away. They moved to the outskirts of the parking lot, where Jerry and Lauren got into a waiting car. Eddie moved to the driver's seat and sped off with the van and Gary.

Meanwhile, Agent Kelly had arrived promptly to the Moran residence. Donna, as instructed, showed him to Gary's room. Sitting on his desk was a note and Gary's notebook of evidence. Agent Kelly picked up the note and began to read:

Agent Kelly,

By the time you read this note, I will have just been kidnapped. In the notebook on my desk are the identities of the kidnappers. This is the same crew who killed Carlos, and probably involved in all your other kidnappings. You have to stop all international flights out of Miami, Fort Lauderdale, and Palm Beach Airports. You know the leader, Gerald Hall. You will find the location of where I am being held in the Everglades in my notes. Also, send someone to stop the breakdown of their equipment at their office, 527 Las Olas Blvd., Fort Lauderdale, at Suite 505. Please forgive me for not including you in my plans. I had to do this for Carlos.

After reading the note, he handed it to his associate and said, "Call Fort Lauderdale Police and have them get a couple of cars over to that address to stop anyone there from dismantling anything, and save all the equipment."

Donna was on the phone to call her mother, without results. She then called Coach Lewis, who was luckily at the school and close by. She read him the note that the agent dropped on the desk, and he told her keep trying to get in touch with her mother and he would be right there. In the meanwhile, Agent Kelly called to hold all international flights and dispatched units to each airport to pick up Gerald Hall. He also set up a helicopter to pick him up to get Gary.

As Agent Kelly left the house to await the helicopter, Coach Lewis arrived. After identifying himself and discovering the game plan that was to ensue, he told Kelly that he was going with him.

"I can't allow you to go along," Agent Kelly informed him.

"Excuse me, sir. You are going to attempt an impromptu rescue. As a retired Special Forces commando, I'm better able to handle this than you are. I'm going with you, and that's that!"

As the helicopter set down, Agent Kelly had no choice but to agree. "Let's go!"

As the men took off to save Gary, Mom, Aunt Connie, and Carol arrived home. Donna ran into her mother's arms, crying and totally scared for her brother's life. Gary had always been big on his scheming, but never to this extreme. He did all of it in front of everyone, and no one knew. At that moment, she prayed that her father were watching over Gary. Carol, also in tears, climbed into her sister's arms as she broke away from her mother.

"Gary's gonna be okay," Donna said as she consoled her little sister. "He has a notebook full of research inside. He had this all planned out. You know how his plans work out." A small smile appeared on her face as she said her last statement.

They all followed their mother into the house. Donna quickly picked up the phone to call Steve. After she hung up with him, she called Michelle to let her know what was going on. At first, Michelle dropped the phone when she heard the initial news that Gary allowed himself to be kidnapped but then realized it was her job to tell her sister about what had happened to her boyfriend. She hung up and grabbed Patti and rushed to the car.

"Where are we going?" Patti said.

"Gary's house," she responded. She then started telling her what had happened as Patti quickly fastened her seat belt.

"Hurry. Get there!" Patti retorted. She, too, was scared of the situation and felt that was where she needed to be.

As they arrived, the house was already surrounded by the Riverside Police Department. Donna had run out to let Michelle and Patti in the house to await news.

CHAPTER 33

Gary woke up in total darkness. His eyes were covered, and his hands bound with rope. He was lying on his side on a dirt floor. He felt no breeze, so he surmised he was inside a structure. He knew where he was. It happened just like he figured. He had begun to struggle to free himself when he heard a noise and quickly stopped moving. He heard a door open, and someone entered the room. As the person approached him, Gary took a noticeable breath. The man stopped briefly and then reached down and picked Gary off the floor and set him down on a nearby chair.

"I know you're awake. Do what I tell you and we won't hurt you."

He sat quietly and listened as he heard the man move around the room. He heard a cabinet door open and close. The man made no attempt to be quiet. This confirmed his location. He knew where he was being held. Soon he heard the man move toward him. He tensed up with anticipation of what was to happen next.

"This is what's going to happen. I am going to untie you. Do not make any attempt to get off this chair or remove your blindfold. I set a timer for ten minutes. When you hear it go off, you can remove the blindfold and you are free to move around the room. There is water and food in the refrigerator, and a bathroom in the far corner of the room. Do not try to leave this room. It's not safe. I will be back tomorrow after your mom pays the ransom we asked for. When I get back, I will knock on the door three times. You have ten seconds to get back to this chair and put back on the blindfold. You're a smart kid, so you know what happens if you see what I look like. Right?"

Gary did not answer him. He felt a hand grab his throat and throw him to the floor. The man picked him back off the floor and sat him again on the chair, where he again felt the hand grab his throat.

"I'm not someone you want to piss off. I said right?"

"I understand what you want me to do, sir. Please don't hurt me," Gary responded.

"Good. Just do what I say and you will come out of this just fine." He went behind Gary and untied his hands. He put the rope on the back of the chair and walked out of the room. Gary heard the door being locked and began to relax. He just had to wait now for the good guys to get there.

As Eddie was on the way back to the dock, his phone rang. It was Miguel. "What's up? You start breaking everything down?"

"That's the problem. There are cops banging on the door, wanting me to let them in. Somehow they found out about us. I tried calling Jerry. I got no answer."

"That little bastard! He seemed too calm. You're on your own, Miguel. Sorry." And he hung up the phone. He quickly spun the boat around to head back to the island in the swamp, throwing his phone in the water as he sped away. He got back to the island, and without knocking, he burst through the door. Gary was walking around and surprised with his entrance.

"What did you do, you little shit? You knew you were being kidnapped, didn't you?" he asked as he grabbed Gary and threw him across the room.

Gary, remembering his football training, rolled and was back on his feet quickly. He was close to the door and made a dash for it. Eddie was fast, though, and caught up with him right outside the door. As Eddie grabbed his shoulder, Gary was close enough to him and did what he did best. He kicked him in the groin, like a field goal. As Eddie backed away and went to his knees to endure the pain, Gary ran at him and drove his shoulder into his attacker's chest, with Eddie and Gary falling at the water's edge.

Without any other warning, an alligator came out of the sawgrass and clamped down onto Eddie's head and quickly pulled him under the water. As Gary got to his feet, he heard a hissing sound behind him. He turned to see two gators approaching him. They were closer to the shed door than he was, so he turned and made a beeline for the airboat. He made it in time, just as the first gator started to climb on board. He climbed to the top of the airboat tower and into the seat. He looked at the ignition, but no keys. They must be in Eddie's pocket. He looked over toward Eddie, and all he could see were legs popping up from the water as he was in the grips of the gator's death roll. He was stuck. He had to wait for Agent Kelly to come and rescue him.

As they approached the swamp, Coach Lewis called out on his headset. "I know where he's at. We went fishing out here last Saturday. Gary wanted to check out this old research shed. Turn northeast past the fishing camp. There are power poles leading to it."

As they approached the site, there was Gary sitting on top of the airboat. As they got closer, it was apparent that they could not land due to the gators, and although armed, they did not want a chance of hitting Gary by mistake.

Coach Lewis, without hesitation, grabbed a harness and slipped it on. "Lower me down," he called out. Agent Kelly looked at him quizzically, but before he could say anything, he heard, "Have you ever jumped out of an airplane or rappelled down a mountain?" With that, he nodded okay and helped hook up the guild line to Coach Lewis. Grabbing a second harness, he stepped off the helicopter rail, heading toward the scared boy below.

Imagine Gary's surprise seeing his coach coming down to get him.

As the coach landed on the seat next to him, he slipped the harness on him and clamped it on his. He wrapped his arms around Gary, and they were whisked off the airboat and were flying through the air. They were brought over to the fishing camp, where there was an ambulance waiting to check Gary out. By the time the helicopter landed, Agent Kelly received word that they had picked up two of the subjects at Fort Lauderdale Airport and one at the downtown office, where they had confiscated all the tech equipment. And with everything Gary had put together, they should be able to bring the suspects to trial. They then reboarded the helicopter for the ride home.

Wildlife officers had to euthanize the gators in order to recover the headless body of Eddie from the swamp.

As they flew away, Gary looked down and said, "For Carlos."

CHAPTER 34

It was impossible to land next to the house with all the cars that lined the street. Word of what Gary had done was spreading rapidly, with TV crews onsite to broadcast the events as they unfolded. It would not be long before the story went national. They opted to fly to the school instead to land, and a car was dispatched to pick them up from there.

As Gary left the car, news crews surrounded him, throwing every question imaginable. A horde of police officers moved in to make a corridor to the house, pushing back the news crews and onlookers. He finally made it to the front door, where his mom was waiting, and he collapsed into her arms. His sisters followed and grabbed onto him.

As he broke from their embraces, Donna said, "Dad was really with you today!"

"Dad was there all the time through everything, but he saved me." He pointed to his coach. "You should have seen it, Mom. Coach Lewis swung down from a cable from the helicopter, picked me up on the airboat, with gators all around me, and pulled me out of there. He never let go!"

His mom was impressed with her boyfriend at that point. No one had told her about how he was saved. She went over to Charles and thanked him for being there to save her son.

Patti was standing back and waited for the best time to approach Gary. But she couldn't wait any longer; she pushed her way through the crowded living room and lunged into his arms, wrapped her arms around him, and in front of everyone, kissed him. As she broke her embrace, she then punched him in the arm. And it was not a light punch.

"Gary Moran, if you ever pull a stunt like that again, you will not be able to walk when I get through with you!" she screamed.

Gary just stood there, clutching his arm in total shock.

Everyone was silent for a couple of seconds. Then the silence was broken by Donna, who started to laugh and blurted out, "Gary always picks his girlfriends by the ones who can kick his ass." She was referring to the time when Lynda scratched him. He picked up on the reference, but for a different reason.

"Mom, you have to give Lynda's dad a call and tell him they can come home now. It's a long story. I will tell you about it later."

He turned back to Patti and said, "I guess I deserved that. I'm sorry for what I put you through. All of you. I didn't want to include anyone in my plans."

He put him arms around Patti as she had calmed down, though a bit shaken still from her outburst. "I'm going to my room now to relax. I'm exhausted." As he walked to his room, he grabbed Patti's hand, and she had no choice but to follow him.

He sat down on his bed, and Patti sat down next to him.

"About Lynda. I had asked her to take pictures of the crowd to see if I could get a picture of them. She did, but she was confronted by one of them, who didn't want his picture taken, and she was harassed for it. Her father moved her and her mother out of state for protection."

"Thanks for telling me. She must still like you for her to put herself in that much danger."

"She does, a little, but it's over between us. We got into a fight last summer before I moved, and she scratched my neck."

"Oh, that must have hurt."

"Not as much as that punch you gave me. I'm going to have a bruise there for a month."

"Sorry," she said with a smile.

Gary lay back on his bed with Patti climbing in next to him. Holding her in his arms. He fell asleep, with her following his lead.

Donna and Michelle peeked in the room to check on them and found them both asleep in each other's arms.

"See, he's a Boy Scout," Donna quipped at the sight. She silently closed the door, so as not to wake them up. After all, her brother did have a busy day.

His mother and aunt Connie did what all Italian women do with a household full of company—they cooked. Other than all the immediate family, Steve, Coach Lewis, there were also Michelle and Patti, and Father Tim had stopped by when he got the news. The crowd out front had dissipated, except for two local news crews who were still hanging out for more of the story.

Gary and Patti emerged from the room an hour later, still half-asleep, except Gary's nose was being awakened quicker as he smelled his mom's cooking in the air. Donna couldn't contain herself to not comment on her brother's position earlier.

"That's a whole new meaning to sleeping with someone I have ever heard of, little brother," she whispered to Gary.

"Shut up!" he responded. He did admit to himself that it wasn't bad waking up with Patti lying next to him. He was just a bit embarrassed that his sister saw it.

They all sat down to eat. The conversation was plenty, but no one mentioned anything about the kidnapping or Gary's planning of it. It wasn't until Father Tim pulled Gary aside after dinner.

"You know that we need to talk about all this, and I don't think it should wait until January for us to talk about it. I asked your mother to bring you by school tomorrow. I know it's Christmas break, but we need to talk. Okay?" Father Tim said sternly.

"I will be there," Gary responded.

"I am glad you are safe. You gave us all a scare," Father added.

"I know, and I'm sorry. It was something that I had to do," Gary replied.

As Gary returned to the impromptu get-together due to his actions, he felt that there was something he had to do. He picked up his glass of ice tea and called out for everyone's attention.

"Everyone! A toast to the true hero of the day, Coach Lewis. If not for him, I'd be lunch for the gators instead of having dinner with all of you!"

With that, everyone raised their glasses of whatever they were drinking for the coach.

The coach responded, "Thank you, and, Gary, if you think you are getting off that easy, wait for practice next season. I have a lot of laps along with other special drills for you."

"As long as it doesn't involve flying over the Everglades suspended from a cable attached to a helicopter, bring it—oops, maybe I shouldn't have said that in front of my mom," Gary said for the comeback.

Mom's look showed she was not pleased.

CHAPTER 35

The next morning, Gary's mom dropped him off at the school for his meeting with Father Tim. After the mutual greetings, they sat down to talk.

"Gary, you do know what you did was very dangerous and, I hate to say, stupid," Father Tim started.

"Yeah, I know, but once I got started, I couldn't stop. They killed Carlos. They had to be caught."

"But why did you have to do it? Why couldn't you collect all the information about them and turn it all over to the FBI?"

"The only way to get a sure conviction was to catch them in a kidnapping."

"Where a man lost his life. How are you dealing with that?"

"He was going to kill me. I had to fight back. Besides, I didn't kill him. The gator did."

"And now the gator is dead. You didn't think this all through, no matter how smart you might think you are."

"Not that smart, I guess." Gary didn't think Father Tim was going to get down on him like this. He was getting a little pissed off.

"Do you think your father would be proud of you about all this? You could have been killed."

"Yeah, but I talked to my dad all through this. He was at my side during all my research. Knowing he was there was what gave me the confidence to get it done."

"He wasn't there to save you at the end, was he?"

"No, he wasn't, but he sent Coach Lewis in his place. I looked up…to the heavens, and there he was. He makes my mother happy. He saved me. He brought me home to my mom and my sisters, and to Patti. Sometimes when you look into the heavens, you miss things that are right in front of you. Coach Lewis was there for me. I got revenge against the people who killed Carlos, and I am alive today to tell you about it. I am smart enough to know where I'm at today. I'm feeling pretty good," Gary said with conviction.

CPSIA information can be obtained
at www.ICGtesting.com
Printed in the USA
BVHW071014180423
662562BV00005B/232